You've connected.

danger.com

@4//Hot Pursuit/

25 Years of Magical Reading

ALADDIN PAPERBACKS
EST. 1972

First Aladdin Paperbacks edition December 1997

Copyright © 1997 by Jordan Cray

Aladdin Paperbacks
An imprint of Simon & Schuster
Children's Publishing Division
1230 Avenue of the Americas
New York, NY 10020

Library of Congress Cataloging-in-Publication Data
Cray, Jordan.
Hot pursuit / by Jordan Cray. — 1st Aladdin Paperbacks ed.
p.   cm. — (Danger.com ; 4)
Summary: When seventeen-year-old Ryan brags about his abili-
ties to hack into protected
computer systems, he finds himself the target of both the FBI and
a cyberterrorist group.
ISBN 0-689-81434-8 (pbk.)
[1. Computers—Fiction. 2. Adventure and adventurers—
Fiction.]
I. Title. II. Series: Cray, Jordan. Danger.com ; 4.
PZ7.C85955Ho 1997
[Fic]—dc21   97-23503
CIP   AC

danger.com

@4//Hot Pursuit/

by
jordan.cray

Aladdin Paperbacks

VISIT US ON THE WORLD WIDE WEB
www.SimonSaysKids.com/net-scene

//prologue

Encryption coded e-mail communication, 27 April.

To: JereMe, CircleK, WannaB, NancE, Topcat33, Komodo5, Hypertex, SonoBoni, LuddMan, Dano50H, HiBob, Quark5

From: MasterGuilder

Re: Millennium Caravan
       Meeting Agenda

Before the meeting (2 B @ quad A/site 3), all core Caravan members should formulate new recruitment ideas/strategy and be prepared to discuss same. List of possible targets will be discussed. Prime target plan formulated (see below).

Parameters for Prime Targets:

1. youth (under 35, media/computer culture incubation)
2. intelligence
3. access to computer network passwords (includes hackers, coders, security personnel, managers, etc.)
4. socially estranged (i.e., misfits)

Procedure:

1. track schedule (trail for several weeks, if possible)
2. appear benign (approach as friend: observe weather/common irritation [ATM line, slow bus service, etc.])
3. offer small service or favor (soda, newspaper, pick up meal check, etc.)
4. gain trust
5. talk ideas (Guild precepts disguised as questions/philosophies)
6. go for agreement (don't lecture; use questions, not statements)
7. break down defenses (the key word is love—flattery, encouragement, praise)

8. *separation from family/friends (under-mine connections/offer better alternative)*

9. *bait the hook (offer power only the Guild can provide)*

Remember, there is no time limit! The above can take months, days, hours, depending on vulnerability of subject. Use yr judgment.

The Caravan Is Supreme.

The Power of the Caravan Increases with Each Member

The Key Word Is Love

Elimination of Enemies Is Necessary and for the Good of All

Encryption coded e-mail communication, 28 April.

To: JereMe, CircleK, WannaB, NancE, Topcat33, Komodo5, Hypertex, SonoBoni, LuddMan, Dano50H, HiBob, Quark5

From: MasterGuilder

Re: Caravan Meeting Results

Meeting of 4/27 resolved the following:

Prime Target's Name: RYAN CORRIGAN
Online Address: Catcher80
Caravan Member Contact: JereMe
*Caravan Member Support: Dano50H and
    HiBob*
Caravan Backup: Komodo5

FIND AND APPROACH SUSPECT

GAIN TRUST

FAILURE IS NOT AN OPTION

you've got mail!

To: All cyberheads@cyberspace.com
From: Catcher80 (Ryan Corrigan)
Re: once upon a gigabyte . . . .

Did you know that hackers were able to access the computer system of the United States Defense Department 162,500 times out of 250,000 attempts in just one year?

Did you know I was one of them?

Call me a hacker. Call me a geek, a nerd, or a loser. I don't care. Ask me why I break into a system, and I'll shoot the answer right back at ya:

Because I can.

High school is just marking time for me. I've managed to make enemies of almost all my teachers. Probably because I let them know that I am way smarter than they are.

The problem is that I've already been accepted at The School of My Choice, and I can't wait to shake the dust from this cruddy burg of Nowheresville, North Carolina, and head west to California. But my mom decided that I needed to stay in my high school for the "social integration," like the prom and senior class day and all that teen crud I could care less about.

So first, I called up my college and asked them if I needed a high school diploma to start classes. They said nah. That's when I made my plans.

Project: Get expelled from school.

It was easy. I hacked into the school computer and shut down the electrical system. This, as you might imagine, really ticked off the principal. But the town paper called and wanted an interview, and I said why not? The trouble was that I guess I got a little cocky and kind of mentioned to the reporter that I'd also hacked into the Defense Department. Not only that, I spilled my future plans to become the person to finally invent a counterterrorism device to foil any attempts to fool with the national electrical power grid.

Problem: The brain-dead reporter who was only half listening to me (strictly a nondigital type) got it wrong. He printed that I had already learned how to hack into the grid.

Well, perhaps I had exaggerated a tad. But I was just trying to get his attention!

Result: Within a day, Men in Suits were knocking on my door. But that was just the beginning of my problems. Because I was soon the most popular guy in town—and the international cyber terrorist poster boy.

Not to mention the target of a seriously scary bunch of smart nuts who just happened to have a target date for taking over the world.

Think I'm exaggerating again? Read on.

1 / / hoopla

"French toast," my mother said, "is not going to save your sorry butt, buster."

"I have fresh blueberries," I said.

She folded her arms. She was in her robe, and her short dark hair was all mashed on one side. She peered at me over her glasses. "Keep going."

"Whipped cream," I said. "Real whipped cream."

She looked at the bowl suspiciously. "Not a nondairy, nonfat, air-puffed soy product?"

"Extra thick, heavy cream," I promised. "And I whipped it myself."

Mom sank into her chair with a sigh. "All right. You're almost forgiven."

I started to whistle as I poured the egg mixture into the hot pan.

"But you're still grounded," Mom added, picking up her orange juice.

Oh, well. You can't have everything. Maybe after she actually tasted some lightly browned, fat-filled fried bread, she'd relent.

I picked up the spatula. The smell of butter and eggs filled the kitchen. French toast is my sole culinary accomplishment. My mom usually melts like butter at the sight of it. But this time, I had messed up in a major way, and I had a feeling that even French toast with blueberries couldn't buy me back my MTV privileges.

Shutting down the school's electrical system was much worse than the other bonehead moves I'd pulled. For example, back in Minneapolis, freshman year, I had created a false ID for a student named Doug Weewe. I enrolled him in classes, gave him allergies in the nurse records, even made him pay a fine on overdue library books. Then, I'd say to kids, "Hey, you seen Doug?" or, "That Weewe—what a cool guy." Soon, Doug was known all around school for his ultrahip wardrobe and his habit of scarfing down Cocoa Krispies right from the box. The major babe of freshman year, Melissa Manders, swore she'd dated him in junior high. Doug Weewe became a person, and nobody had ever met him.

I considered running Doug for class president, but I was younger then, and I couldn't figure out all the angles. Then Mom decided she hated her job working for a landscape gardener—I mean, duh, a landscape gardener in *Minneapolis?* There's fifty feet of snow on the ground for, like, eleven months! So we got the maps out and Chiquita-ed, which is what we call picking a new town and splitting (like a banana, get it?).

I bet that Doug Weewe is in that Minneapolis high school yearbook, three years later. Chess Club 1, Spirit Booster, Future Farmers of America. Motto: I've Fallen and I Can't Get Up. Favorite Movie: *The Invisible Man.*

Ha!

But enough nostalgia. I'm getting too sentimental. Right here and now, in Nowheresville, North Carolina, I was in deep doo.

Mom picked up the paper with a sigh.

"I just hope the wire services don't pick up your story," she said. "It will be in papers all over the country. The whole world will come knocking on our door."

"Don't you want to be on *Oprah*, Mom?" I asked, flipping the toast.

She looked at me over her wire rims. "No."

"Everybody wants to be on *Oprah*," I said.

I'm not sure what the big deal was to my mom. With our family existence, a little turbulence was the rule, not the exception.

I put French toast topped with blueberries and whipped cream down in front of Mom. I poured her coffee and added warm milk.

"This is a bribe," she sniffed, picking up her fork. She ate her first bite and rolled her eyes. "I love bribes."

I put my plate down and grabbed the syrup pitcher before she drained it on her own French toast. I was just cutting my first bite when the doorbell rang.

Mom looked at me over her fork. "Who

could that be? It's only seven-thirty in the morning."

"Publisher's Clearinghouse?" I suggested.

Mom smiled nervously as she put down her fork. She tightened her robe sash and headed for the front door. I left my breakfast and trailed after her.

She opened the door. Three men in bulky navy suits stood on our porch.

"Mrs. Grace Corrigan?"

Mom's voice sounded completely calm. "That's right."

The tallest man flipped open a badge. "FBI."

Mom gripped the door handle tightly. She seemed to sway for a moment. Then she opened the door wider. "I guess you'd better come in, gentlemen," she said in a shaky voice.

Then, the men saw me. The tall one fixed me with a glance that was way too serious for so early in the morning.

"Ryan Corrigan?"

I nodded. I noticed that I was still holding a forkful of French toast. Syrup was dripping on the carpet.

"What do you want with him?" Mom asked, wheeling around.

"Where's your computer, Ryan?" the tall man asked.

"Leave him alone!" Mom said.

"We have a search warrant, ma'am," the tall man said.

"For what?" Mom demanded. Her hands were shaking, and she stuck them into the pockets of her robe. "What are you looking for?"

"Computer crimes division, ma'am," the agent replied. "We're here to investigate your son."

Mom let out a shaky breath. "Ryan?"

"My computer is in my room," I said. I pointed. "But the school said they weren't pressing charges—"

They all ignored me and headed in the direction of my room. One of the men took out a portable tape recorder and said, "Entering suspect's bedroom."

I was a suspect? But of what?

Mom looked at me. Her eyes were wide behind her glasses. "What should we do?" she whispered.

I looked down at my fork. I licked the syrup off my hand. "Eat?" I suggested.

They packed up my computer and took it. They took all my floppys. They took my CD-ROMs, every single one, even the encyclopedia and the games. They took my notebooks from school, and they took my sci-fi paperbacks.

Then, they asked me questions.

How did you access the national power grid?

How many times did you hack into the Defense Department files?

What online addresses do you use?

Have you ever corresponded with Jeremy?

"Jeremy?" I said. "Never heard of him."

"JereMe," the tall agent answered, spelling it out. "It's an online address. How about MasterGuilder? Are you in touch?"

"Master Who?" I said.

The tall agent fixed me with his most severe I-Am-a-Fed glance. "We've got your hard drive, Ryan," he said softly. "So it doesn't make any sense not to cooperate."

"But I *am* cooper—"

"How about the Caravan?" the tall Fed asked.

"Is that a rock group?" I said.

"The Millennium Caravan," he repeated.

"Oh, a *New Age* rock group," I said.

The tall Fed pressed his thin lips together. "Have you been contacted or have you contacted the Millennium Caravan?" He pushed the tape recorder closer to me.

"No," I said. "I've never heard the name before."

"Has JereMe ever mentioned the Millennium Caravan?" he asked.

What a stupid trap. These guys were so transparent, it was scary. Don't they know that everybody watches TV?

"I've never heard of JereMe," I said.

"I want a lawyer," Mom said suddenly. "This has gone far enough."

"Your son could be in jail right now," the tall Fed told her.

"He's a minor," Mom said, standing up. She was about half the size of the tall guy. But she didn't flinch. "And I won't let you question him any longer without a lawyer present."

The agents all exchanged glances.

"We have what we want," the tall agent said. "For now."

"We'll be back," the shorter one said.

"Hey, looking forward to it," I said.

Mom squeezed my arm so that I'd shut up. The men in suits went out to the van, where thousands of dollars of my state-of-the-art computer system were now loaded.

Mom closed the door and sank onto the floor, just like that. Her robe pooled around her.

"Oh, Ryan," she said. "I thought—"

She put her hands on her knees and bent her head. She took several long, deep breaths.

"It was scary," I said. "I'm sorry."

I wanted to sit on the floor next to her, just to keep her company. But I perched on a chair. We were not, at this moment, pals. She must have been seriously, severely angry at me for this.

When Mom looked up, she was frowning in concentration. It was her planning face, not her angry face. "We have to change our plans," she said, rubbing the bridge of her nose.

"What do you mean?" I asked nervously. She looked so intent and scary.

"I'm putting you on a plane to California," Mom announced. "You're leaving town ASAP."

"But, Mom," I said. "Don't you remember? I'm grounded."

2//hooey

Mom was definitely in panic mode, and nothing I said made any difference. Like, I'd already committed to a summer job at the computer store. And that she'd already put down a deposit for a week on the beach at Jekyll Island. Or even that I hadn't done anything really wrong, so the FBI wouldn't arrest me.

She didn't listen. She just kept rubbing her nose in that way she does when she's freaked. She told me to pack. Then she sat at the kitchen table and arranged my immediate future.

She called someone in California and left a message. They called back a few minutes later. She talked for a long time in a low voice in her bedroom. I couldn't hear a thing. I didn't even know she had a friend in California.

"Of course you do," Mom told me when she finally got off the phone. "Lily. I've talked about her. We went to school together. She has an extra room in her house. It's a great old Victorian. You'll love it."

"So this woman I've never met is going to let me live in her house?"

"Just for the summer," Mom said. "She lives in the hills near Palo Alto, which is where you'll be in the fall. You'll get to know the area. She's even got a little Volkswagen bug you can tool around in."

"But what will I do all summer?" I asked. I pictured myself, living in an isolated house with some old lady. I didn't think I should say "old lady," because if Lily had gone to college with Mom, they'd be the same age:

"You'll do what you do here," Mom pointed out. "You can get a part-time job, if you want. And Lily works for one of those high-tech companies out there. She knows more than you do about computers. She's got a PC you can use."

I nodded. The setup was beginning to sound slightly more interesting. At least I'd be wired.

"You're flying into Los Angeles," Mom told me. "Lily will pick you up. She'll meet you right at the gate."

"Los Angeles? Isn't that kind of far from San Francisco?"

"It's the only flight I could get," Mom told me. "You leave tomorrow morning."

I looked at her doubtfully. It was the middle of the afternoon, and she was still wearing her robe. Her hair wasn't mashed on one side anymore, but it was all messed up from her raking her fingers through it every five minutes.

"Don't you think you're hitting the panic button a little too hard?" I asked.

"I didn't like those men," Mom said, crossing her arms. "You're only seventeen, Ryan. I'm trying to protect you."

"But they're the FBI, Mom," I said. "They can track me down in about two seconds, probably. If they want to."

"I don't think they'll be that diligent," Mom said, looking for her purse. "At least, I hope not. You're just leaving for school a little early, that's all. Now, I have to get to the bank. We're going to pay cash for your ticket."

"Don't you think you should change first?" I pointed out.

She looked down at herself. She laughed for the first time that day. "What am I going to do without you?"

"Be arrested for excessive pajama wearing," I said.

For as long as I could remember, Mom and I had been a family of two. My dad died in a car crash when my mom was pregnant with me. Totally tragic, right? I guess Mom had been devastated, because she moved to a new town. Then, when I was only about two, she moved again. She must have liked the pattern, because we didn't stop.

Nine different schools in nine different states. When you change schools that often, there are two possible ways to cope. Either you become really good at making friends, or really bad. I took the latter route. After a while, you just get sick of having that hopeful, befriend-me look on your face, so you substitute an I-don't-care look. Then, a little time goes by and you realize you really *don't* care.

Everybody sort of circles you like a pack of wolves, trying to sniff out your cool factor. Since I've always been tall and skinny and I have this truly ridiculous strawberry-blond hair, you can imagine how low I scored.

When I was a little kid, I didn't realize how truly weird it was to move almost every year. I thought it was a complete gas to sit at the kitchen table with a pizza and get out the map. I'd always want to move to places with names that sounded like amusement parks, like Ho-Ho-Kus, New Jersey, or King of Prussia, Pennsylvania.

As the years went on, my lack of social skills grew to a truly dysfunctional level. I was not, as one might say, user-friendly. But then I got my first PC, and everything was jake. I bonded with hardware and software, and started thinking of people as hard drives with attitude. It helped.

Mom had a tendency to go ballistic when I referred to people as hard drives. "You've got to open up," she kept telling me. "You've got to trust people."

"The last time I trusted someone was in

seventh grade," I'd told her. "Randy Pallidan suggested we trade locker combinations and be best friends. Like an idiot, I agreed. When I got there after lunch, my combination was spray painted on my locker, and all my stuff was on the hallway floor."

"Oh, honey," Mom told me just the other day. "You won't always be the New Guy. I promise. And you'll do great in college. Tastes change. Babes like brains. Especially in Palo Alto. Geeks there drive Porsches and fight girls off with a stick."

Mom was doing her best to cheer me up. But I didn't have my hopes up. When you get your hopes up, you lose. My motto: Trust no one. Travel light.

"Does this mean you're buying me a Porsche?" I'd asked.

As soon as Mom left for the bank, I took off on my bike. I rode around the quiet streets aimlessly for a while, just to make sure I didn't have any FBI agents on my tail.

Which, when I thought about it, made me feel totally, randomly surreal, like I'd stepped through the TV into a dumb cop show. *I* had to worry about being tailed?

It's amazing how life can go from normal to truly weird in about ten seconds flat.

When I was sure I wasn't being followed by the bad guys, I rode to school. Classes were in session, so I sneaked in the side door. Hoping I wouldn't run into Mrs. Dragoneer, the vice-principal who prowled the halls twenty-five hours a day and who was called, of course, Dragon Lady, I headed for my locker.

I spun the combination and opened it. I let out a sigh of relief. My laptop was still there. The FBI hadn't thought of everything.

Tucking it into my knapsack, I headed out of school without seeing a soul. It was strange to walk through the halls, passing classrooms I'd filed in and out of for two years. I glimpsed Peyton Delaney's blond hair through that little window in the door. I'd had a serious crush on her junior year, but she'd treated me as if I had a communicable disease. Burt McCallister sat in the back row, his meaty face creased in concentration as he tried to simulate brain function.

Once, he'd stolen my jockstrap—my jock-strap, how weird is that?—in the gym lock-er room and used it as a slingshot to send my sneakers into the shower. I'd walked through three periods with wet feet, leading to a brief period of being nicknamed "Squishy."

In other words, I would not miss high school.

Short-circuit the electrical system? They're lucky I didn't blow the place up.

Packing was not difficult. I upended my T-shirt and sock drawers into a suitcase, then threw in two extra pairs of jeans and sneakers. I'd wear my hiking boots on the plane. Done.

Then I fired up my modem. Mom still wasn't home. She was probably buying me travel-sized toothpaste, mouthwash, Band-Aids, and shampoo. She considers travel-sized packaging one of the great innovations of the late twentieth century.

My mailbox flag popped up as soon as I signed on. I clicked on the icon. It was a let-ter from JereMe! That was the address the Feds had kept grilling me about.

How weird was that?

I sat there for a minute. JereMe was obviously not just another e-mail buddy, looking to chat. Should I access the mail, or not?

The thing about cyber space is, no matter who flames you, or makes you angry, or scares you, you're fairly well protected. All you have to do is switch off your computer. So what harm would it do to check out what JereMe had to say? I clicked on.

Ryan,

Okay, hold on. First weird thing. How did JereMe know my real name?

When the Feds get you in their sights, you're toast.

Okay. Second weird thing. How did he know the Feds had targeted me? It had just happened that morning!

Need protection? We are all cyber heads out here, seeking like minds. Want help, just ask.

JereMe

"No thanks," I said, deleting the mail with a click. Like I needed any more trouble from the men in suits!

Then an "instant message" box popped

up on the screen. I'll give you exactly three guesses who it was from.

I shouldn't have clicked on. But like I said before, you figure you can always turn off the computer, right?

Look, I don't want to spook you, buddy, JereMe wrote. *Probably the Feds ran my name by you. But they're probably running* your *name by someone else as we speak.*

He had a point.

One day, you're minding your own business, doing a little harmless hacking, and the next thing you know, your setup is kaput!

So I wasn't alone.

I hear you, I wrote back. *I had a sweet system, and now the Feds are probably playing some lame CD-ROM game on it.*

LOL, Jere wrote, which stands for Laugh Out Loud and basically means, I get the joke. *The Feds are just getting up to speed digitally. The average hacker knows way more than they do. Don't ever forget that. They're strictly analog. We're digital!*

But they have the stinking badges, I wrote.

Point taken. But true power is found in knowledge. So we win. Think about it, Catcher. There's lots of hackers out there getting pushed around. I'm part of a group that decided to push back. We're not illegal—just smart. It's a cool group, and we're inviting you to join. Check out our Web site—we're the Millennium Caravan.

Millennium Caravan! That's the group the FBI mentioned. What if they weren't harmless hackers? What if JereMe was selling me a load of hooey?

I'll check it out, I tapped out. Which is the equivalent of "Maybe we can get together on Saturday."

Cool, JereMe wrote. *So, we noticed your national power grid access. You have impressed the unimpressables, dude. Care to share a few details?*

None to report, I answered. *The reporter wanted to sell papers. He totally exaggerated.*

Okay, I hear you. You're afraid to tell me the truth. But the Feds aren't listening now, my man. You're talking to a fellow hacker. I've hacked my way into some tight places myself. Remember the hacker code, dude—

information should be shared. We're all on the same side, right?

I'm serious as swine flu, I wrote. *I've hacked into a few systems, but not that one.*

Yeah, the school electrical system—way to go!

Nothing to it, I said modestly.

Don't kid a kidder, bud. Cyber space is like the Wild West. We're all cowboys on this frontier. But if we don't watch out, we'll have fences and border patrols. In a digital universe, access should be universal. Doncha think?

Sure, I wrote. *Give me a home where the gigabytes roam.*

LOL. So where else did you get root access? Any online services?

JereMe was starting to spook me. Suddenly, I felt pumped for info. A creepy sensation made my hairs stand on end, like someone was in the room with me and had just breathed onion fumes on the back of my neck.

Whoa. You're a fast mover, I wrote. *We just met. I'm not so ready to share.*

No problem. I'm just curioso. So, have

you seen any coming attractions for summer movies? There's a whole bunch of sci-fi headed for your multiplex. What looks good?

Suddenly, we were chatting about movies. Was JereMe trying to put me at ease? That spooked me more than anything.

I haven't kept up lately, I wrote. *But I gotta disengage now. Nice chatting with you.*

I started to sign off, but suddenly, JereMe's words flashed in front of my eyes.

Okay. But remember—we have friends everywhere, if you need us. Even in California.

Whoa—weird thing number three! The paper had mentioned I was going off to college, but not where. I hadn't told anyone, in fact. Mostly because nobody was interested.

I had that weird sensation again.

How did JereMe know I was leaving for California?

3//time to Chiquita

Still there? JereMe prompted.

Why California? I typed out.

Sorry if I spooooooked you. But we masters of the digital have to hang together, my man. Cyber life is the ultimate freedom, doncha know? I just want to keep up the dialogue with other hacker snackers—even if you're not a serious hacker, you still like a taste now and then.

I really have to sign off now, I typed in.

But words popped up almost instantaneously. *First, let me convince you that California is not for you. Second, let me tell you why you should let me convince you. Our caravan of digital devotees has root access to systems you can only dream of—just for fun, not profit! For example, the FBI's Most Wanted. What if you were on their Ten Most Wanted List? Wouldn't you like to erase your name and info?*

I swallowed a lump in my throat. *But I'm not on the list,* I wrote. *All they did was question me.*

Maybe the FBI hasn't put you on the list. But what if another group had root access? What if they could?

I couldn't make sense of what I was reading. So I just typed out *?????*

Just yanking yr chain, dude, JereMe wrote back. *Wouldn't it be cool to be Most Wanted for, say, a day?*

Are you telling me that your Mill Car could do that? Or would? I wrote back, spooked.

Could, most def. Would . . . I dunno. That's why cyber space is dangerous. In the wrong hands. The Wild West, remember?

My mouth felt dry. I tapped out, *What do you want from me?*

Just your ears. That's all. Why don't you agree to listen to what we have to say?

Because I don't like being threatened, I wrote.

Awwww. Relax, bro. I'm your friend.

But I was tired of JereMe. And I was severely allergic to someone who called me "my man."

So this time, I didn't say good-bye. My finger snaked out and turned off the power. JereMe's words disappeared in a blip and a beep.

I sat, staring at the blank screen. Maybe Mom was right. Maybe it was time for me to blow town. One thing I knew for sure— I wouldn't tell her that JereMe had contacted me. She was already too nervous about my being known as some kind of Super Hacker.

Besides, I was freaked out enough for the both of us.

Mom and I stood by the airport ticket counter. We had booked my seat and checked my suitcase. We had found out which gate I would be leaving from. But Mom kept staring at the departures screen above our head, so I knew she was trying not to cry.

"Gate six," she said for the second time. "It's down that way. We can stop for magazines and candy—"

"Mom," I said, interrupting her. "No offense, okay? But I'd rather you didn't go to the gate. Just say good-bye here. Why torture yourself?"

She tried to grin. "I guess you don't want any cute babes seeing me hugging and kissing you and calling you my sweet baby boy."

"You got it," I said.

She took my face in her hands. Her eyes filled with tears. "My sweet baby boy," she said, her voice all choked up.

"Mom? Uh, scene?"

She dropped her hands. "Right." She cleared her throat. "So. You have your ticket?"

"Got it."

"Carry-on luggage?"

"Roger."

"Lily's number, just in case you miss her at the airport?"

"I won't miss her at the airport, and I have her cell phone number. I also have her home number, her fax number, and her e-mail address. Are you sure you don't want to give me her social security number?"

"Why I'm going to miss such a wise guy, I can't imagine. You'll call when you get there?"

"First thing."

Mom's eyes filled with tears again. "I really think this is the right thing to do."

"I know."

"I'll come out and see you soon."

"Yeah."

She hugged me. She told me she loved me, which was unfortunate, because I choked up, too. I felt about eight years old, even though she only came up to my shoulder.

"24/7," she said.

"24/7," I answered. It was what we always said. That we were there for each other twenty-four hours a day, seven days a week.

"Well," she said, giving me a wobbly smile, "time to Chiquita, I guess."

"Make like a banana and split," I said.

"Okay," Mom said. "I'm going now."

"Right," I said.

She gave me another quick, tight hug, then wheeled away, walking quickly.

"Mom!" I called.

She turned around. Tears were running down her face.

"You're going the wrong way!" I said. "The parking garage is that way." I pointed.

She hit herself on the side of the head and made a comical face. Then she turned and headed in the right direction.

I stood for a minute, watching her. I was seriously worried about her ability to get along without me.

The gate was crowded. I craned my neck over the bodies and piles of luggage, looking for a seat. How come everybody complains about flying, and nobody stays home?

Finally, somebody moved a piece of carry-on luggage the size of a foot locker off a seat at the end of the row. I scooted over and nabbed it. Then the person next to me got up, so I even had elbowroom.

I took out some candy and flipped open my computer notebook, planning to play some computer chess. But whoever had gotten up had left the latest issue of *Digital* on the seat next to me, so I snatched it up.

On the first page, a big yellow Post-it was stuck over the photograph.

DON'T GET ON THE PLANE. YOU NEED US, RYAN. WE'RE HERE FOR YOU. NOT LIKE MOM, WHO SENDS YOU THREE THOUSAND MILES AWAY WITH A HUG. FORGET THOSE M&M'S. PEANUT, RIGHT? WE'RE THE REAL THING.

I stared down at the M&M's in my hand. They were peanut M&M's. I thought about Mom hugging me for so long by the ticket counter.

The Millennium Caravan was watching me.

I looked casually around the gate area. I don't know what kind of person I was looking for. A geeky guy with a plastic pocket protector? A Bill Gates look-alike?

The M&M's spilled out over the floor as I stood up. A little girl walking with her dad pointed to the floor and said, "Candy!" She bent over to pick one up, but her father told her not to, and she started to wail.

So much for not attracting attention.

I tucked my notebook under my arm and reached down for my carry-on bag. But as I leaned over, I was bumped from behind. I felt my notebook being slipped out from under my arm.

"Hey!" I whirled around. I could see a tall figure in an army fatigue jacket and baseball cap moving away from me down the corridor.

I took off after him. He was fast, but I was just able to keep him in sight through the crowd. I danced around a group of flight attendants wheeling their suitcases. One of those long pedestrian trains that carries tired people from gate to gate made a turn in front of me, and I had to race to cut it off. The driver yelled a surprised "Hey, buddy!" at me, but I kept on going.

I was gaining on the guy. He had just as many obstacles as I did. He tried to jump over a luggage cart, and he clipped his shin. That slowed him down long enough for me to dodge a family wearing Disney World hats and throw myself at his ankles.

So much for being laughed off every gym team since junior high!

I had his ankles, but he kicked so hard that I lost my grip. I reached out with one hand and managed to grab my laptop. But I couldn't keep my hand on the thief and the laptop at the same time, and he scrambled away. He jerked to his feet and dashed off. I still hadn't seen his face.

I heard a commotion behind me, and two security guards broke through the small crowd that surrounded me. I let out a sigh. Help at last.

"What's going on here?" one of the guards asked.

I opened my mouth to explain. But I didn't get a chance. A bystander in sunglasses and long brown hair pointed at me.

"He's a thief!" she cried. "He stole that laptop!"

The next thing I knew, I was dragged off.

4//the suits

"I'm telling you, I'm not the thief," I told the airport security officer. "I'm the one who almost got ripped off."

I'd already told him this ten times. As they picked me up off the floor. As they walked me down the hall. As they led me back into the part of the airport nobody sees and into a little room with a carpet the color of olive loaf. They closed the door.

"Why are you taking one witness's word for it?" I demanded. "She didn't see anything except me tackling the guy. Wouldn't you tackle the guy who stole your computer?"

I seemed to be getting through. A flicker of doubt showed on the security officer's face. But mostly, he just looked bored. I guess he was disappointed. He probably spent his time hoping to catch some dastard-ly terrorists, or maybe an international jewel thief, not a skinny teenager with a laptop.

"Okay, kid," he said. "Settle down. We'll get it all straightened out. What did you say your name was?"

"Ryan Corrigan," I said.

"How old are you, Ryan?"

"Seventeen," I said.

His gaze flicked over me. "Yeah? You look older."

"I'm tall for my age. Look, you can call my mom. But she's probably not home from the airport yet," I added. "She just dropped me off." We lived about a half hour from the airport, and, knowing Mom, she had probably gotten lost.

"Let's give her a few minutes," the officer said. His entire face suddenly elongated, and his eyes squinted. I thought he was making a funny face, or maybe transmuting into an alien being. But he was suppressing a giant yawn.

I almost apologized for keeping him awake on the job, but for once I was smart and kept my mouth shut.

The officer clicked a few keys on his computer. I saw his eyes move over the screen. This time, he didn't bother restraining his yawn.

But suddenly, his mouth snapped shut. He tried not to show a reaction, but his body stiffened. With exaggerated casualness, he swung around on his chair and stood up. He stretched.

"I'm gonna go get a cup of coffee. Soda?"

"Sure," I said.

As soon as he was out of the room, I swung his monitor toward me. He'd exited from whatever program he had going, but he was no match for me. Leaning over, I clicked a few keys to access the last program he'd been in.

The FBI logo popped up on the screen.

Uh-oh.

The Ten Most Wanted List stared me in the face. The name GuildMaster was number one. There was no photo. He was described as a cyber terrorist with no known address. His real name was not known, either.

I scrolled downward to see the next

name. A familiar face appeared. Mine. It was my high school yearbook picture, so you can imagine how geeky I looked.

All my stats flashed in front of my eyes, along with the information that I was wanted on charges of cyber terrorism, kidnapping, and grand theft.

Kidnapping? Grand theft?

I blinked. I read it again, slower this time. This wasn't a stupid mistake on the part of the FBI. This was deliberate misinformation.

Was that what JereMe was warning me about?

Maybe the FBI hasn't put you on the list. But what if another group had root access? What if they could?

This was the work of the Millennium Caravan! They wanted to prove to me how powerful they were.

That's why cyber space is dangerous. In the wrong hands.

My brain whirled like a wobbly merry-go-round. I couldn't seem to think clearly.

Why had they set me up? Hadn't JereMe said something about putting me on the list for a day?

I heard footsteps approaching. All I knew was that I had to get out of there. I grabbed a paper clip off Sergeant Yawn's desk. Quickly, I unbent it.

I sat back down. Right near my knee, I spied an electrical outlet. I unplugged the desk lamp and wrapped the paper clip around the prongs until they touched. As the officer opened the door, I stuck the plug back into the outlet.

ppppffffzzzzzz!

Everything blew—lights, computer, fax. The entire office short-circuited.

"What the . . . ," Sergeant Yawn said.

It was only five steps to the door. I covered them in two.

5//casing the joint

I lucked out. A tour group was milling around the baggage area when I burst into the main part of the airport. The group was led by a distracted guy who kept yelling, "All together! Are we all together?" while he checked his list, lost count, and had to start again.

It was easy to lose myself among them. We all filed out to the curb outside, where the bus was waiting. Every time the guide tried to count the bobbing heads, I moved around. Everyone was trying to keep track of their luggage, talk to each other about the bumpy flight, and look at a map at the same time.

I made it onto the bus and took a seat at the back. The guide gave up trying to count heads and slumped into a seat with a sigh.

We took off with a lurch toward downtown.

I checked behind us every once in a while,
but no flashing lights appeared. Twenty
minutes later, we pulled up in front of the
Holiday Inn. I got out with the rest of the
group, then beat a hasty retreat while they
charged like bulls toward the reception desk
while the guy yelled, "Wait—let's form a
line!"

It was about a fifteen-minute walk to my
house from downtown. We lived off one of
the grassy squares in an old neighborhood.
Mom had found the small carriage house in
the paper. It was once a stable attached to a
big mansion. The mansion was now an
apartment building that fronted the square.

I planned my walk so that I would end up
on the far corner of the square near a big
old oak tree. There was a Civil War monu-
ment next to it I could duck behind.

Everything looked quiet. People were
walking their dogs, or reading the newspaper on a sunny bench. A guy across the
street was cutting the lawn in front of the
apartment building that fronted our car-

riage house. As I watched, the machine strangled on something. The guy shut off the mower and went around to check it out. A rock. He picked it up and tossed it into the bushes.

It was just an ordinary day. Relief flooded through me. I could go home. Mom would know what to do. I would tell her everything, and she'd hire a lawyer, or call the police, or do whatever she thought was right.

I started across the square. But then I noticed something. The guy cutting the grass was wearing shorts and brown shoes. Geeky business shoes, with hard soles. Who would cut their lawn in good shoes?

An FBI agent, that's who.

My house was being watched. I took two steps backward, turned and walked off. I had to discipline myself not to run like a rabbit.

No one followed me. There was just one problem.

Where was I going?

I walked and walked. I thought about

calling Mom, but I figured our phones must be tapped. And what if the guy in the brown shoes was with the Millennium Caravan, and not the FBI? What if I put Mom in danger?

Mom hadn't been so paranoid after all. She must have figured that the story of my cracking the national power grid would make me a target. No wonder she'd insisted on secrecy. No wonder she'd tried to get me out of town. She'd paid cash for my plane ticket, and hadn't told anyone but Lily where I was going. I bet she'd even deliberately chosen L.A. because it was a big airport, where it would be harder to trace me.

I stopped suddenly. Mom's plan had been a good one, so why shouldn't I follow through on it? Why shouldn't I just head out to California?

But I wouldn't fly. I'd take the train, or a bus. I would find one of those cyber cafés and e-mail Lily that I'd be arriving on a different date and would contact her. I'd ask her to tell Mom what was up.

Then, when I got to Lily's, I'd have a computer system with plenty of juice. I'd either find a way to hack into the FBI myself and erase my file, or make them an offer over the Net. I'd explain what had happened and tell them I'd help track down the members of Millennium Caravan.

Because I shouldn't make the mistake of underestimating the group. They had targeted me because they thought I could help them. I had to prove that I couldn't, somehow.

All I had to do was find a ticket office and get a refund for my ticket. Luckily, I had kept it in the pocket of my denim jacket. I fished it out and opened it up.

It was stamped NONREFUNDABLE.

Great. Now I was stuck. My traveler's checks were in my carry-on luggage, which was still sitting at gate six. I had about forty dollars in my wallet. How far would that get me, Tennessee?

I had practically no money, no clothes, and no computer. I couldn't call my mom. The FBI was after me, so I couldn't call the police.

I was sunk.

6//waiting to inhale

I have another motto: When you don't know which direction to take, inhale junk food. Personally, I am convinced that someday, scientists will discover a link between grease and advanced brain function.

I was in an unfamiliar neighborhood, so I had to walk a few blocks before I found a diner. It looked a little run-down, the kind of place with centuries of grease on the walls, and those cracked leatherette booths. Perfect.

The diner was deserted, which didn't exactly indicate good things about the food. But I was not in a position to be choosy. I picked a booth near the door that had a view out to the street.

I ordered the cheeseburger platter and an iced tea, and passed the time reading the signs that hung over the grill, like WHEN MY SHIP COMES IN, I'LL BE AT THE AIRPORT and EVERYBODY HERE BRINGS GOOD CHEER: SOME COMING IN, SOME GOING OUT. Was this place the Cornball Café?

The waitress delivered my cheeseburger platter, and I was just digging in when the little bell over the front door tinkled.

A girl gave me a bored glance and headed for the counter. She was almost my height, with shiny black hair that was twisted into a loose braid that hung almost to her waist. She wore a faded olive green T-shirt and paint-splattered black jeans. A denim shirt was tied around her waist.

She ignored me, but I was used to that behavior from girls. I went on eating as she ordered the cheeseburger platter and a diet soda from the waitress.

She swung her stool to the side so that she could cross her legs. She had very long legs. I watched her boot swing back and forth. Back and forth. Then I felt courageous enough to sneak a peek at her face.

Mistake. Our eyes met. Hers were the

color of denim that had been washed about fifty million times. They were startling next to her black hair and tanned skin.

She looked away quickly. I felt myself blush, which is this truly annoying habit that could lead to my jumping out a plane without a parachute one day. I reached for the ketchup and pounded on the bottle. Nothing came out. The bottle was empty. I looked up for the waitress, but she was busy at the back making a phone call.

Who needs ketchup, anyway?

I took a bite of cheeseburger and stared at the NO SPITTING, ESPECIALLY IN OUR FOOD sign.

From behind my shoulder, a ketchup bottle was gently placed to the left of my plate. I looked up, and the girl was standing at my elbow. "Thought you could use this."

"Fries just aren't fries without it," I said, picking it up.

"It's the mixture of salty and sweet," the girl agreed. "And these are the best fries in town."

"Do you come here often?" I asked. When I heard my words, I wanted to stuff fifty French fries into my mouth at once. What a stupid pickup line!

But she didn't seem to notice. "Every day, just about. I go to the art school down the street." She nodded at my plate. "It's wise to stick with the simple stuff. Once I tried the moussaka. It was a decision I'll regret for the rest of my life."

She said the words solemnly. But then she grinned, and I laughed. The waitress came out of the kitchen holding the girl's platter.

"You want this here?" the waitress asked, pointing to the counter.

The girl hesitated. A voice inside me, a voice I usually ignore because it is always, always wrong when it comes to girls, said, *Go for it, Ryan!*

"Would you like to sit down?" I asked. My voice cracked a little.

She grinned. "I hate to eat alone."

She signaled the waitress and slid into the seat opposite me.

Okay, I have to pause here and repeat myself. A gorgeous girl had just sat down opposite me. And it was her own choice.

It was turning into quite a day.

The girl wasn't your classic gorgeous, I guess. Her nose was kind of big. But her eyes and her full lips made it all come together in her face, somehow. She didn't look like anybody I'd ever met.

She took the ketchup bottle and poured a lake of it onto her plate. She was wearing three wide silver bracelets that clinked together whenever she moved her hand.

"I'm Sabrina Seringo," she said. She ate a French fry.

"Ryan Corrigan," I said before I realized that maybe I shouldn't.

"Do you go to the art school, too?" she asked.

"No," I said. "But I'm really interested in art."

Yeah, right. Mom tried to drag me to museums. But my idea of art was a Superman comic.

She nodded and took a bite of her burger. When she swallowed, she said, "I'm a photography major, actually. I'm really interested in digital photography. It's a whole new field, just starting to be explored."

How do you like that. I meet a gorgeous arty babe, and she's *digital!* Talk about luck!

"I don't know much about digital photography, but I'm really into computers," I said. "What do you mean, exactly?"

Sabrina looked wary. "Are you really interested?"

"Totally," I said.

"Whoa," Sabrina said. "You're going to regret this." Then she smiled.

She filled me in on the digital possibilities of photography while we ate. She talked about color and perspective and image. She waved her cheeseburger around while she talked, and took enormous gulps of her diet soda. I liked her better and better.

I have to confess something. I've been basically honest about my lack of success with the girl species. But it isn't totally their fault. It isn't as though they overlook me just because I'm not the handsomest stud muffin in town. It's also because when I start to talk to them—or should I say, attempt to talk—I do things like tie and untie my sneakers, continually tug my earlobe, or tuck and untuck my T-shirt into my pants. And I do it completely unconsciously. The whole time I'm fidgeting, I say words I would never say when I'm not in girl mode. Things like, *whoa, you know?* and *awesome, awesome, awesome!*

In short, I do not do face well.

So the fact that I was sharing lunch with a girl, and actually stringing words of more than two syllables together, was pretty amazing.

"I wish I could show you some examples of what I'm talking about," Sabrina said as she slurped the last of her diet soda. "The thing is, I just moved out of my dorm for the summer session. Everything's packed up and in storage."

"Drag," I said. "But I'm heading out of town anyway. I think."

"What do you mean?" Sabrina asked. She reached over for a napkin, and I could see the golden tan skin of her throat at the V of her T-shirt.

I answered quickly, before major blushing resulted. "I'm supposed to be on a plane to California right now," I explained. "I missed my flight. I'm putting off telling my mom. She'll go ballistic."

It was all basically true. I'd just left out about eighty percent of the story.

"I'm sure she'll understand," Sabrina said. "Or not. What am I saying? My mom would freak. She could jump into the ring with Conan the Barbarian and win."

I grinned. "Plus, it was a nonrefundable ticket. And we're not exactly rolling in the stuff."

Sabrina nodded. "You should travel the way I do—on the cheap. I'm headed to California, and I don't have to pay a cent."

"What's your secret?" I asked curiously.

"Baby-sitting," Sabrina answered. "It's not my favorite thing—well, it's about as far from my favorite thing as you can get. But all I have to do is wipe noses and read storybooks to twins for about ten days, and I end up in sunny San Diego for the summer. My mother lives there now."

Sabrina reached over and snatched my last fry. She swirled it in ketchup. "This couple, the McDoogles, are friends of friends of my mom. They're fairly dorky, but who cares?" Sabrina ate the fry. There was a tiny blob of ketchup on her lip. She scooped it off with her tongue.

"If you run into any more McDoogles, let me know," I said, watching her. I never thought watching a person chew could be so fascinating.

"There's only one McDoogles," she said. "Thank goodness . . . wait! I'm about to be brilliant. Why don't you come with me? The McDoogles have this huge RV monster, so there's plenty of room. They pay for all food and expenses. And originally, they told me I could bring my boyfriend." Sabrina made a face. "Fortunately, we broke up before I asked him. What do you say?"

I hesitated. I didn't even know this couple. And Mom would probably freak.

"Believe me, I could use some normal company," Sabrina went on. "The McDoogles are these terminally cheerful chipmunk types."

But it sure would solve all my problems. I would make it to California without spending a cent, first of all. But the best part of all was that I could just disappear.

Sabrina looked at her watch. "We're supposed to leave in about an hour. I was just fueling up on some junk food. Twyla isn't the greatest cook. Do you want to come and meet them?"

"Sure," I said. "Why not?"

7//boomers

Sabrina waited outside while I stopped in a cyber coffee shop called Totally Wired to send an e-mail to Lily. I told her that I had decided to take a slower route to California, but that I was fine. I told her to tell Mom not to worry.

Fat chance of *that*. But at least I'd be in California in less than two weeks, so she wouldn't have to worry for too long. And I'd try to send Lily another message along the way.

I tagged along while Sabrina picked up her duffel bag from the dorm lobby, and we headed for the McDoogles.

The house was not hard to spot. A massive RV sat in the driveway, and suitcases were piled on the grass. A slightly overweight middle-aged couple dressed in

Hawaiian shirts and shorts stood looking at a map. They each had sandy hair and freckles and very white skin. They waved frantically as they saw us approaching.

"Bree!" they cried together.

"It's our very own Charlie's Angel!" the woman added.

"Warning," Sabrina muttered to me. "If you ever call me Bree, I'll throw you out on the highway."

We walked up, and Sabrina introduced me.

"So this is the boyfriend, Sabrina," Twyla twittered. "Ooh, he's a tall one."

"How's the weather up there?" Bud chortled.

"I know I said I wasn't going to ask him," Sabrina said. "But Ryan's plans changed at the last minute, so I was wondering if he could hitch a ride."

"Ab-sa-tively!" Twyla trilled.

"Pos-a-lutely," Bud said. "Glad to have you aboard the McWanderlust!" He patted the RV.

"The more the merrier!" Twyla agreed.

"It never rains, but it pours," Bud added.

"Now, you have to meet Kaylen and Kyle," Twyla said. She turned toward the house and screeched, "Kaylen! Kyle! Come here this instant!"

Two miniature versions of Bud and Twyla ran down the driveway. The eight-year-old twins were dressed identically in orange T-shirts and green plaid shorts. They had identical short haircuts. I couldn't tell which was a boy and which was a girl. I didn't think I'd ever be able to tell them apart. They both politely shook my hand, then ran off again.

"They love people!" Twyla said, beaming.

"So, son, where's your luggage?" Bud asked me. "I'm just about to stow the gear."

"Everything is in here," Sabrina said, pointing to her overstuffed duffel. We had talked on the way over about my lack of luggage and decided to say that we were sharing a suitcase. Sabrina had plenty of oversized T-shirts for me to borrow. On the way, we'd ducked into a drugstore and I'd bought a toothbrush and two packages of underwear. "Travel Light" was my motto, remember?

I helped Bud load the RV while Sabrina arranged the kids' candy, comic books, and stuffed animals within grabbing distance. Twyla organized tapes in the front seat while she yelled instructions to Bud about where every suitcase should go. He had to unpack three times because she forgot to mention that she'd need the little red plaid suitcase, or the yellow nylon bag. But at last, we were packed and ready to go.

I took my seat next to Kaylen and Kyle. Sabrina sat next to me. Twyla sat in the big captain's chair in the front, and Bud slid behind the wheel.

He backed out of the driveway carefully. Familiar streets flashed by as we headed for the highway. I had a momentary panic—was I doing the right thing? I didn't know these people. All I knew about Sabrina was that she loved ketchup. I wasn't used to trusting people.

But I didn't have to trust any of them, I told myself. I just had to ride along.

Bud and Twyla pulled on matching baseball caps, and the sign for the highway heading west appeared. I felt a spurt of excitement as Bud pulled onto the on ramp. I was really going!

As soon as Bud was cruising safely in the right lane, Twyla turned and waggled a cassette tape at us. "Ready?"

"For what?" I said. Next to me, Sabrina gave a low groan under her breath.

"I hope you know the words!" Twyla told me over her shoulder as she popped in the tape.

The theme from *The Love Boat* boomed through the vehicle. Twyla and Bud sang each word. Even the kids knew it!

Come aboard, we're expecting yeeewwwww!

"I didn't mention this major drawback," Sabrina whispered to me. "But the McDoogles are major TV hounds. Old TV shows from the sixties and seventies. They have a tape of all the theme songs."

The Love Boat theme ended, and the theme from *Gilligan's Island* began. Bud and Twyla began to harmonize.

Sabrina winced and looked out the window. One of the twins—either Kaylen or

Kyle, I wasn't sure which—started whining for candy.

Okay. Being trapped in a recreational monster vehicle with two singing baby boomers and twins who could whine in an identical key wasn't my idea of paradise. But at least we were on the move. How bad could it be?

8//beam me up, Scotty. . . please!

By Memphis, Tennessee, I was wondering if earmuffs would drown out the sound of TV themes. By Arkansas, I was ready to jump out of the moving car into traffic.

The McDoogles gave "chipper" a bad name. Their mouths were always moving. Either one of them was reading aloud from a guidebook called *Fun Facts About Our Great Nation* as the other one drove, or they were singing along with the six-tape series, *Favorite Classic TV Tunes*.

Somewhere between Arkansas and civilization, I began to wish I was carsick, just for a distraction.

"I'm really sorry, Ryan," Sabrina told me at our campsite one night. "I didn't know they were *this* awful. I owe you. Big time. They are truly weird."

I made the *Twilight Zone* doo-doo-doo-doo noise, and Sabrina winced.

"Please," she whispered. "Promise me. No more theme songs. Ever."

"Sure, Bree," I said, and she punched me.

But not only were Bud and Twyla orbiting the planet, Kaylen and Kyle were the strangest kids I'd ever met. They were so boring that they drove me crazy. They played "capitals" for hours. Or else they'd hum these tuneless, rhythmless songs to each other. They were the White Noise Twins.

By Oklahoma, I decided that I'd rather lick the bathroom sponge than be trapped in the McWanderlust another second. If the *Enterprise* were orbiting Earth, I would beg to be beamed up, no question.

The McDoogles had one redeeming feature, however. They served as a bonding ingredient between Sabrina and me. Every time Twyla started singing, or Bud read another Fun Fact, Sabrina and I would exchange glances. And I didn't mind exchanging glances with the prettiest blue eyes on the planet.

Each evening, when we pulled into a campsite, Sabrina and I would volunteer to do all the chores. We went for fresh water, we found wood for a campfire, we even did the laundry if the campsite had facilities. Anything to escape the madness.

I discovered on these evenings how alike we were. We agreed on movies and music and books and the superiority of Cheerios over every cereal known to man. It was a true mind meld.

One night, Sabrina gave me her version of high school. We were in the laundry room, washing towels. Sabrina was perched up on a washing machine, munching on pretzels.

"Listen, if you think *your* high school years were bad, you should hear about mine sometime," she said, pointing a pretzel stick at me. "I spent *months,* make that *years,* trying to fit in. And then I had this revelation. After high school, I wouldn't give these bozos the time of day. What was I knocking myself out for?"

"High school *makes* you want to fit in," I said gloomily. "Even with people you despise."

Sabrina just snorted. "It's in the water. They pump it through those water fountains near the gym. They get you all hot and sweaty and thirsty, and then inject you with chemicals that destroy every brain cell that's programmed for independence and creativity. That's why the geeks survive high school the best—they sit out gym class." She snapped a pretzel stick in two. "They don't drink from the fountain."

I laughed. Sabrina handed me a pretzel stick.

"The coolest kids in high school are *never* truly cool," she went on. "They're the ones who end up in dead-end jobs with no lives. It's the misfits who go on to do things. Look at history. I bet Napoleon flunked geometry. Heck, I bet he flunked French," Sabrina said, her blue eyes dancing.

"So what was so bad about your high school years?" I asked her.

Sabrina chomped thoughtfully. "Well, my dad is a hippie holdover, first of all. I was born in Berkeley, California, and we moved around a lot."

"We did, too!" I said. "Almost every year

when I was in grade school. How many states have you lived in?"

"Seven," Sabrina said. "No, eight! I forgot Montana."

"Nine," I said modestly.

"Aw, you beat me."

"Only because of that three-month stint in Wisconsin," I said.

Sabrina jumped to the floor and took the towels out of the washer. I helped her load them into the dryer. Then we hopped up on the machines again. We swung our feet, bumping them gently against the sides. The door to the laundry room was open, and the night air smelled sweet. Life wasn't so awful all of a sudden.

"That's probably why we bonded so quickly," Sabrina said. "It was kind of cosmic, the way it happened that day. I felt like I knew you already, or something. I really felt that we shared some kind of *connection*."

"Well, I know that we shared ketchup," I said. "Not to mention French fries. You kept stealing them from my plate."

She grinned. "Then I owe you."

Sabrina held out the bag of pretzels. I

took one. The washer felt warm underneath my legs, and our feet made pleasant thumping noises as they swung. It was a tiny moment. But I felt something shift inside my chest, and I realized, maybe for the first time, that there was a reason I had a heart.

It was like switching from copper wire to coaxial cable. In a heartbeat, a major shift in consciousness occurred. My linear logic processes blew into bits. *Poof.*

Have you ever looked at a lightbulb and seen the filament glow? Hot orange surrounded by cloudy pale glass. Wattage suddenly makes sense. It has a color.

Love was like that. Sabrina glowed next to me. She gave off heat as well as light. If she were a power source, they'd have to devise a whole new system of measurement. No more 100-watt bulbs—there would only be laser light SABRINAS.

The very next day, destiny stepped in. We'd driven through most of Oklahoma when it happened.

Bud finally rebelled against Twyla's food. "Not fried bologna sandwiches again!"

he exclaimed when Twyla told him what was for lunch.

"With butter and ketchup, just the way you like them," Twyla said in a hurt voice.

"Ewwwww," the twins chorused.

"That's it," Bud said. "Honey, I'm not complaining about your cooking. I swear I'm not. But I've got to get me a steak. We're stopping for lunch."

"But where?" Twyla wailed. "We're in the middle of nowhere. I don't trust these fast-food restaurants."

Like they could possibly have any worse food than what came out of the RV's teeny kitchen.

"There!" Bud said, pointing to a billboard. There was a picture of a happy family eating pie while a black-and-white dog begged for scraps. Written across the bottom in red were the words BLUEBONNET CAFÉ—WHERE HOME COOKIN' HITS THE SPOT!

Bud stepped on the gas, and we made the café just in time for lunch. We were the only ones there, and we all ordered the blue plate special, fried chicken and mashed potatoes, except for Bud, who got his steak.

The food was delicious. The waitress set down a frosty pitcher of iced tea. We were all so grateful for the good food that the whole family chowed down without a word. The waitress went back to watch TV with the cook.

I buttered my corn bread and took a big bite. It had been so long since I'd had decent food. I was going to make this lunch last forever. The waitress had already informed us that second helpings were free.

The sound of the TV was turned way down. A show called *You Can Catch a Crook* was on. The waitress was folding napkins, not paying attention. The cook yawned and picked up a comic book.

I cut a piece of chicken and ate it. I closed my eyes in bliss. When I opened them, I was staring right at the TV. And I saw my geeky yearbook picture.

I was the crook on *You Can Catch a Crook*!

The waitress still sat folding napkins. The cook was concentrating on his comic book. At our table, everyone was concentrating on their food. That was lucky. But all one of the McDoogles had to do was look up, and they'd see my face on screen.

"Yeeeowww!" Bud suddenly cried, leaping to his feet. Twyla had reached for the butter and spilled her entire glass of iced tea in his lap. "That's cold!" he said, pushing away from the table. His plastic glass toppled over, and his tea spilled on Kyle. Kyle started to wail, too.

"Oh, my!" The waitress picked up a towel and hurried toward us. As she ran, I slipped on my baseball cap and pulled it down over my eyes.

The segment must be almost over. I was going to escape detection. No one had noticed the TV. But from now on, I would have to be extra careful. I'd have to stay out of sight when we stopped for gas, or pulled into a campsite.

Then I noticed Sabrina. A chicken leg was held aloft in her hand. She was frozen, staring at the TV. She dragged her eyes away and looked at me. A look of shock was on her face, and a slowly dawning horror.

She knew!

9//everybody gets the pie

Sabrina rose so abruptly, her chair hit the table behind her.

She didn't meet my eyes. "I—I—have to—need some air," she finished in a rush. She bolted away from the table.

The waitress looked up. "But what about dessert, honey? There's pie."

I stood. "I need some air, too." I rushed after Sabrina.

"But everybody gets the pie!" the waitress yelled after us.

I caught up with Sabrina halfway down the lane that ran on the side of the restaurant. I held her arm, and she yanked it away from me.

"Get away from me!" she cried.

"Sabrina, wait," I said, trying to keep up with her. "Just let me explain—"

She whirled around to face me. "Explain

what? That you lied? That you're a wanted criminal? That you aren't who you said you were at all?"

"But I am the same person!" I exclaimed. "I'm exactly the same. I just got in some trouble, and it wasn't my fault—"

"Yeah, right," Sabrina said, tossing her braid behind her shoulder. "And everybody in jail is innocent."

"Can't you just listen to me?" I asked. "I thought we were friends."

A flicker in her pale blue eyes told me that I'd just gotten through—a little.

"Five minutes," I said. "I can explain it all in five minutes."

Sabrina looked at her watch. "Start talking," she said.

It took ten, but she didn't stop me. Her expression slowly changed. After a minute or two, she stopped asking questions and just listened. Something in her face told me that I had gotten through.

Finally, I ground to a halt. "Do you believe me?"

She shook her head slowly, but I could tell she didn't mean no.

"I guess I believe you, Ryan," she said. "But it's all so hard to swallow. The Millennium Caravan—it just sounds goofy. And how could a group hack into FBI files?"

I shrugged. "I don't know how. But I've hacked into some pretty secret places. The FBI already considers these guys dangerous."

"What do they know about them?" Sabrina asked. "Do they know where they're based, or who the head of the group is?"

"They only know his e-mail address," I said. "GuildMaster."

"It sounds like a computer game," Sabrina said. "Not like something *real*. So what are you planning to do?"

"I'm going to try to erase my name from the FBI files, first of all," I told her. "I have to make sure that the Caravan didn't plant evidence against me. They could have set me up with real crimes."

"I guess," Sabrina said. "But they sound like a bunch of hackers, not a bunch of criminals."

"Who knows what they are," I said. "All I know is, I have to get to California."

Sabrina was silent. A breeze lifted a strand of hair that had come loose from her braid. She looked into my eyes for a long moment. Then she took my hand. "I'll help you," she said.

10//rear view

Secrets are secrets. They are something you keep to yourself. They are things you think, or stupid things you've done, that you don't want anyone to know about. And my rule in life was never, ever, to tell anyone my secrets.

But after I told Sabrina everything, I felt about ten pounds lighter. It was like my story had actual weight, as though it were a package that I handed over to her to carry for a while. She tucked it under her arm, and kept on walking.

Most guys find their perfect girl at a club, or on a beach. I found mine while I was on the run from the FBI.

Love. It wasn't what I expected. It didn't unfold in a linear way, like a story. It rushed at you, all at once, in a blur. Nothing made sense, and I didn't care. It was like watching a big stupid Hollywood action movie—you know the story wouldn't make sense if you stopped to think about it. But you're totally excited, completely caught up, and waiting for the next explosion.

Sabrina and I tuned out the McDoogles. We spent the next day concocting a new scenario—after I straightened out the FBI thing, we would visit each other that summer. Then, Sabrina would transfer from her old school to mine.

We spent long, boring Texas highway hours talking while the kids napped and Bud and Twyla read Fun Facts to each other. We crossed over the border into New Mexico, heading toward Albuquerque. The scenery changed as we headed west. Wildflowers dotted the landscape, and at sunset, the rocks blazed red. Even the McDoogles seemed affected by the landscape. They turned off the music and didn't even talk.

"I have a proposal," Bud announced. "I think we should turn off the highway and explore the back roads. It'll set us back a day, but I really want to see the country. Plus, we can hit Santa Fe instead of Albuquerque. Vote?"

We all voted yes. At this point, I was in no hurry.

The purple mountains drew closer. The skies were huge and the clearest blue I'd ever seen. Everyone was quiet as we just drank in the sight.

"This landscape is so incredible," Sabrina whispered to me. "New Mexico is such a spiritual place."

"I hear you," I said. "If it can shut the McDoogles up, it must have some awesome power."

The next morning, I noticed a red pickup truck behind us. At first, I didn't pay any attention. Kyle had made Sabrina and I switch places, so that I was now sitting behind Twyla. I could see the big side mirror on the passenger side. I saw the red truck early in the day. It was there after we stopped for lunch, and it was there after we turned off onto another secondary road.

Sometimes it would disappear, but then it would pop up again, staying well behind. I could never see the driver. The truck had tinted windows.

I told myself I was being paranoid. First of all, I didn't think the FBI would trail me in a red pickup. It would be too conspicuous. But then again, in this part of the country, pickup trucks were the norm. Maybe a red pickup was like a limo in Beverly Hills.

Bud turned off the road for gas. I waited, and a few minutes later the truck zoomed by, passing the station and disappearing down the road.

Paranoia is a dangerous thing. It takes away my appetite. When Twyla suggested we make a junk food run at the convenience store, I didn't even salivate.

"I want potato chips!" Kyle said.

"Me, too!" Kaylen chimed in. "Sour cream and onion!"

"Barbecue!" Kyle said.

"Come on," Sabrina said. "You can both have your own bag."

The kids gleefully ran toward the convenience store. Sabrina paused by the open door. "You okay?"

Behind her shoulder, I saw the empty road. No truck. No one on my trail. "Sure," I said.

Sabrina's mouth quirked in a half smile. "Uh-huh. Talk to me, Corrigan. Something's up."

"Just a minor freak-out," I said. "I thought somebody was following us today."

Sabrina frowned. "A car?"

"A red pickup. It just seemed like it was there, behind us, no matter what we did."

"Maybe they're heading toward Santa Fe, too," Sabrina pointed out.

"I'm sure that's it," I said. "It's just that Bud drives about fifteen miles an hour. Everybody passes us, even little old ladies in Subarus. And this guy was on our tail all day." Sabrina's dark eyebrows descended. She looked worried. She looked over her shoulder and scanned the road.

"I'm sure it's nothing," she said. "Just some tourist taking it easy. It spooked you. That's natural. But you can't get paranoid."

She was probably right. "Thanks for the

reality check," I said. "Now you'd better hustle. Any minute now, Kyle and Kaylen will start screaming. They've reached their patience limit." I looked at my watch. "Ten . . . nine . . . eight . . ."

"Okay, okay," Sabrina said, laughing. "I'm going."

She started toward the convenience store. I jumped out of the RV and took a deep breath of the chilly air. We were at higher elevations now, and the temperature had dropped about ten degrees. We had all pulled on our jackets.

I decided to wash up in a real bathroom, with a real sink, not the tiny Barbie-sized one in the RV. I headed around the corner of the service station and stopped dead.

The red pickup was parked at a hasty angle on the side of the station. It wouldn't be visible from the road, or the gas pumps. And I saw in a glance that the rest rooms weren't on the side of the building. They must have been inside, where the store was.

Which meant that whoever was driving the red pickup was trying to conceal it.

Panic sent every hair on the back of my

neck shooting to attention. I leaped back into the shadows just as the driver's door opened. Every muscle tensed, and I was ready to run.

But the driver just got out in a leisurely, bored way. He stretched his arms toward the sky. Then he put his palms on the roof and stretched his back. He just looked like a regular guy, dressed in dark jeans and a denim shirt, with sunglasses and a baseball cap pulled low.

A bleached-out red baseball cap.

Just like the guy who'd lifted my laptop at the airport.

Then he swept off the cap to wipe his forehead. He had wiry brown hair that frizzed around his face. His features were sharp, but not memorable.

But I knew him. And it wasn't just from the airport. I hadn't seen his face then. But where had I seen it?

He walked a few paces away, stretching his legs. He leaned down, picked up a pebble, and tossed it into the bushes.

And then I knew.

He was the same guy I'd seen cutting the

grass next door to my house, back in North Carolina.

And he wasn't FBI. Suddenly, I knew that deep in my bones. I didn't know much about law enforcement, but I knew that an FBI agent wouldn't be in a little red pickup, traveling alone. He wouldn't try to steal my laptop—he'd just confiscate it. And he wouldn't be that out of shape, either. This guy definitely had a paunch. And by the way he kept stretching, his back was probably killing him.

And if he wasn't an FBI agent, and he was following me, that meant I had someone else on my tail.

Someone from the Caravan.

I hadn't gotten away at all. They'd been behind me all the way!

11//hide in plain sight

So what did I do with this information?

I did what any red-blooded, brave American teen would do. I panicked.

I ran back to the store. Sabrina was standing in front of the snack display with the kids. I signaled her frantically through the glass, then pointed to the RV. Then I took off toward it like a jackrabbit.

A few seconds later, Sabrina slid open the door and hopped inside. "What's up?" she asked breathlessly.

"He's here!" I hissed. "The red pickup is behind the service station. And I recognize the driver! He was staking out my house back in North Carolina. He's the one who tried to steal my laptop!"

Sabrina's mouth dropped open. "Are you

sure?" she whispered, as if the guy were close by.

"Positive," I said.

"Do you think he's FBI?" she asked.

I shook my head. "I think he's from that Millennium Caravan," I told her. "I've got to get out of here! Maybe I can fake stomach cramps, or appendicitis, or something, and the McDoogles can drive me to a hospital. No, wait—you can pretend that we had a fight, and I told you I was going to hitchhike to California—"

"Hold on a minute, Ryan," Sabrina cut in. "Let's not freak out. We have to think."

Sabrina dropped her head in her hands. I watched as her fingers massaged her temples as she thought. Finally, she looked up at me with resolve in her eyes. "Ryan, why should you run? You've got the perfect cover. This guy isn't going to nab you right in front of the McDoogles. He's just tailing you. So let him."

"Let him?"

"Where are you going to go?" Sabrina pointed out. "If we put our heads together, we can come up with a plan between here and San Diego. It's a big state. You can disappear there."

"I guess you're right," I said. "But it's so creepy to think of him back there, watching me."

"I know," Sabrina said with a shiver. "But, Ryan, you're not alone. You've got me."

And then she leaned over and hugged me. I smelled her hair, and felt how strong her arms were. And I felt my heart dance, as though it were inline skating to "Love Will Keep Us Together."

"Let me go hurry the McDoogles along," Sabrina said as she pulled away. "The sooner we get out of here, the better."

I watched through the front window as Sabrina hurried toward the store. I could just see the top of her head as she talked to Bud. She pointed toward the RV. Then she herded the kids—their hands full of potato chips—back to the car.

"Bud had to go to the bathroom," she whispered to me. "We'll take off in two minutes."

"My, my, you kids sure do have ants in

your pants," Twyla said merrily as she buckled her seat belt.

Bud emerged a minute later. He guided the lumbering RV back on the road. I felt better as the miles passed. I kept checking the side mirror, but I didn't see the red pickup. It was almost as though I had imagined it.

But the landscape suddenly seemed lonely to me, as we rose higher and higher in what Twyla had read to us was a "high desert" landscape. I wished that Bud hadn't turned off the main road "to get up close and personal with this magnificent scenery." I wished we were on a crowded interstate, stopping at crowded campsites with noisy kids and barking dogs, because this wild, rugged country seemed like a place where trouble could flare up, and then die away. And nobody would ever know.

"Well, it's getting on to dusk," Bud said hours later. "I'm guessing we'd better stop here. It's not exactly Shangri-la, but it'll have to do."

At first, we thought Kozy Kampgrounds

was abandoned. There were no campers or RVs pulled up in the various spaces underneath the trees. The office door was closed, and the shade was down. But just then a man came out on the porch and squinted at us.

"I guess they're open, then," Bud said. He pulled the RV into a space. Then he headed off for the office.

"We'll light a campfire and get cozy," Twyla said cheerfully. "Let's stretch our legs a bit first."

The twins grabbed a ball and ran out. Sabrina and I climbed out cautiously. We looked up and down the road, but it was empty. I hadn't seen the pickup since we left the gas station.

"You see?" Sabrina whispered. "It's okay."

Kyle tossed the ball to Kaylen. She caught it, shrieking with excitement. She threw it back to Kyle.

I watched the throw idly. It was high. Kyle faded back to catch it. And, out of the mist, I saw the red pickup, speeding down the main road.

It's funny how instinct works. I should

have run the other way. But I could see how fast the truck was moving, and how Kyle was moving backward, not looking, trying to catch the ball, and without even thinking about it, my legs were pumping, and I was shouting, and running straight toward the road.

The red pickup swerved just as I reached Kyle. I grabbed him as if he were a football. I felt his *oof* as the air left his body. He was small for his age, and light, and I tucked him under my arm and fell back. Kyle fell on top of me. My breath left me in a *whoosh,* and I saw the red pickup correct its swerve and zoom down the road.

"Are you okay?" I asked Kyle. He looked as though he was about to let loose with his trademark siren wail.

But instead, another siren sounded. A sheriff's cruiser rounded the curve. He must have been chasing the pickup, but when he saw me and Kyle on the ground, he pulled over.

"My baby!" Twyla snatched up Kyle while Sabrina knelt beside me, her blue eyes full of worry.

"Are you okay?" she asked.

"Ryan, I will never forget this, as ever long as I do live," Twyla said, her eyes streaming tears. "You saved my baby's life."

I found that I could breathe again. "No, I just—"

"Ran out into traffic and grabbed him," Sabrina finished, grinning at me.

"Is everybody all right?" the sheriff asked as he walked up.

I was still sitting on the ground, eye level with his boots. I didn't look up. I prayed he would just go away. I hoped he wasn't a big fan of *You Can Catch a Crook*.

"Everybody's fine, thank goodness," Twyla said as she rocked Kyle, trying to quiet him. "My little boy ran out into the road, and he nearly got hit—"

Kyle nodded importantly, even as tears streamed down his face. "The car came, but Ry—"

"Oh, my baby!" Twyla wailed, clutching Kyle to her again. If she wasn't careful, the kid would die of suffocation.

"Was it that red pickup?" the sheriff asked. I sneaked a peek at him. He was frowning at Twyla.

"I didn't see anything," Twyla said. "I just saw my baby in danger."

"I didn't see the car," Sabrina said. "I was looking in the other direction."

"And you, son?" The sheriff bent over to look at me. "Did you see it?"

"Not too clearly," I said, trying to figure out if I should tell the truth. Well, why not? Why should I protect the Caravan? "But, yeah, it was a red pickup," I finished.

He nodded. He stared at me, long and hard, and I dropped my head again and pretended to dust off my jeans.

"So where are you folks from?" he asked in a casual tone. But my nerves did the hootchy-kootchy dance. This guy might have talked slow and walked slow, but I could see a watchful intelligence in his dark eyes. Muscles strained under his khaki-colored shirt. Leave it to me to land at the feet of Sheriff Sly Stallone.

"We're traveling cross-country," Twyla said. "Started off in North Carolina."

"Pretty state," the sheriff said in the same offhand tone.

Kyle began to fidget in Twyla's arms.

Kaylen was bouncing the ball a few feet away. Twyla lowered Kyle.

"You've got a fine state yourself, here," Twyla told him. "That's why we left the interstate. We wanted to see the country."

The sheriff looked at Kozy Kampgrounds. "Well, there are better places to see, but I reckon you'll find them," he said. He looked at me again as I slowly straightened. "What did you say your name was?"

"Kyle!" Sabrina suddenly yelled. "Kaylen! Twyla, they're playing by the road again!"

Twyla sighed. "Do you believe these children, Sheriff? I'd sure appreciate it if you'd put a scare into them."

"Be glad to," the sheriff said. He walked off with Twyla.

Sabrina stepped closer to me. "Don't tell him your real name," she whispered.

"What?" I asked.

"Just don't," Sabrina hissed. "Why borrow trouble? Listen to me, Ryan. What if he's some gung-ho sheriff who memorizes the FBI Most Wanted List? You've got to deny everything. Say you're David Wallaby, from Seattle, Washington."

"Who?"

Sabrina's eyes followed the sheriff. I looked over my shoulder. He skirted us and went to the car. I saw him checking something on his computer.

"*Repeat what I just said*," Sabrina ordered me fiercely. "Say it. David Wallaby."

"David Wallaby," I said. "From Seattle, Washington. But—"

Her fingers dug into my arm. "Just *do it*," she whispered ferociously.

The sheriff got out of the car and headed toward me.

"What did you say your name was?" he asked me.

"David Wallaby," I said.

"Funny. I thought the kid"—the sheriff indicated Kyle with his strong, manly chin—"started to call you something else."

"Ramjet," Sabrina said. "The kids call David Roger Ramjet. It's a nickname."

The sheriff nodded thoughtfully. "I see. Well, it's probably just a misunderstanding. But it's best to clear this kind of thing up, don't you think? Seeing how you're staying here for the night, that is."

"Actually," I said, "that hasn't been decided for sure."

"Because you fit the description of somebody I should be watching out for," the sheriff said, as if I hadn't spoken. "So I'd appreciate you coming along to the station for a few minutes. Do you think you could do that?"

He wasn't asking me. He was telling me.

So I said okay.

12//incarceration

The building was small and made of cinder block. It was basically one waiting room, with the deputy's desk pushed against one wall near the front door. The sheriff had a tiny office off a hallway that led to the parking lot.

I waited on a hard chair outside the sheriff's office while he went in and closed the door. He was probably calling the FBI.

I tried to smile at the deputy across the room, but he just ignored me. He was a skinny guy with a paunch and a receding hairline that he usually covered with a cowboy hat. I could see the red line across his forehead from where he'd taken it off. His shoes must have been too tight, too, because he'd taken them off and was rubbing his stocking feet. They were needle-toed snakeskin cowboy boots, and I wondered how he managed to chase anyone in them. Then again, they probably didn't get much call for foot chases in Four Guns, New Mexico.

Just then Sheriff Dupree poked his head out and motioned me into his office. "So, David, can I see your wallet?"

"My wallet?"

"Your ID," he answered.

I swallowed.

"I'm waiting," he said.

I reached into the back pocket of my jeans. But my wallet was gone! Puzzled, I reached into the other pocket, then my front pockets.

"Problem?" the sheriff asked. I had to hand it to him. Nothing surprised him.

"I must have left it in the RV," I said. "Or maybe it got stolen."

"I see." The sheriff looked down at a folder on his desk. "I've called the FBI down in Albuquerque. They're sending someone for a look-see as soon as they can. My computer's down. So if you're really David Wallaby, you're in for a wait. And if you're not"—he looked up—"you're in a heap of trouble."

"Just who am I supposed to be?" I said.

"Ryan Corrigan. Some kind of computer criminal. Sound familiar?"

"No, sir, it doesn't," I said.

"Right. Want some coffee while you wait?"

"Okay," I said, even though I don't like coffee. I figured that I should accept his hospitality. Maybe it would soften him up. But somehow, I doubted it.

He poured two cups and handed me one. Black.

"Sorry," he said. "No milk today."

"No problem," I said politely. I took a sip of the hottest, strongest coffee I'd ever tasted. I had a major choking fit, which was embarrassing. But then I figured it might prove to him what a wimp I was. How could I be a hardened criminal if I couldn't even handle a cup of coffee?

But he just gave me a handful of sugar packages and told me to wait in the hall.

I sat in the hall for two hours. It was worse than detention. Maybe the computer really was down. Or maybe he was trying to make me sweat. They always did that to the bad guy on TV.

Of course, I wasn't a bad guy. But the FBI thought I was. Except that I was pretending to be somebody else. So I shouldn't be sweating at all. But I was. The funny thing about a police station is that it makes you feel like Jesse James.

Back at Kozy Kampgrounds, the McDoogles were probably wondering what was going on. They'd promised to wait until everything was straightened out. Sabrina had given me a thumbs-up as the cruiser pulled away.

The sheriff poked his head out. "Shouldn't be too much longer. More coffee?"

"Sure," I said, even though my stomach was still battling the last cup. But at least I could stretch my legs on the way to the coffee pot.

I went into his office and gave him my cup. But before he could pour, we heard a commotion outside.

"But I have to see him," I heard Sabrina say. "Right now!"

There was a knock on the open door, and the deputy stuck his morose face inside. "Sorry to bother you, Rafe. But there's a girl out here, says she's—"

"Sabrina Seringo," Sabrina said, striding into the office. She placed my wallet in front of the sheriff. "David left this in the RV."

The sheriff didn't even glance at it. He just nodded calmly at the deputy. "Thanks, Will, I'll handle this. And put your darn shoes on, will you?" Then he turned to Sabrina. "And you are—"

"His girlfriend," Sabrina said in a voice of great patience. "We're traveling with the McDoogles cross-country. We get free room and board for watching the twins."

"He told me," Sheriff Dupree said, reaching for the wallet and flipping it open.

I shot a glance at Sabrina. What was she up to?

"David's father will be calling you shortly, Sheriff Dupree," Sabrina went on. "He's a lawyer in Seattle. A very important lawyer. He wants to know why his son is being held without being charged."

Sheriff Dupree seemed to be ignoring

Sabrina, but I'm sure he was listening. He wouldn't let her intimidate him, however. He stared at the driver's license in his hand. Then he threw it down, and I saw it clearly. I saw my photo next to the name David Wallaby.

The surprise nearly lifted me out of the chair. Sabrina put her hand on my shoulder.

"Are you okay, David?" she asked. "He didn't hurt you, did he?"

Sheriff Dupree rolled his eyes.

"Well, the coffee *was* pretty hot," I said.

Sabrina shot me a shut-up look. The sheriff tilted his chair back.

"Well, are you going to let him go?" Sabrina demanded, thrusting her chin forward in a way I'd never seen. "Obviously, you have the wrong guy. Not to mention a very angry and very prominent lawyer on your back."

"Can't let him go unless the FBI says okay," Sheriff Dupree said.

"Then why don't you check with them?" Sabrina asked with exaggerated sweetness.

"Computer's down."

"Maybe it's working again," Sabrina said.

Without moving from his reclining position, the sheriff reached over and, with one finger, entered a few keystrokes.

He frowned and sat up. He clicked away at the computer. "Looks like you two are telling the truth. The FBI says to let you go."

I stood up, relieved. "Great! Well, it's been swell. Don't forget to write."

Sabrina shot me another scathing shut-up look. The sheriff was looking at both of us in a way that made me feel like running from the station as fast as I could. He sensed something was wrong.

"Well, thank you, sheriff," Sabrina said brightly.

"Now, hold on a minute," the sheriff said, reaching for the phone. "I want confirmation on this."

"But the McDoogles are leaving soon," Sabrina said. "That's our ride."

"They can wait another five minutes," Sheriff Dupree said, punching out a number.

"Let's give him some privacy, David," Sabrina said, pushing me toward the door.

She kept on pushing, past the chairs and down the hall. The deputy saw us. Sabrina smiled and waved, but she kept moving.

Just then, the sheriff called out, "Keep an eye on those two, Will!"

The deputy looked at us, his mouth agape. He had one foot halfway into his cowboy boot. Obviously, he did not have quick reflexes.

Sabrina looked at me. "Run," she said.

"What?" But she was already yanking my elbow, pulling me toward the door.

I could hear the deputy clattering behind us, trying to run with one boot half on and one boot off. "Hey!" he cried.

But he was clumsy, and we were fast. Sabrina slammed open the door to the parking lot and raced out. I was right on her heels.

There was a black Jeep Cherokee in the parking lot next to the sheriff's cruiser. Sabrina hopped in and fished out keys from her pocket. Where had she gotten a Jeep?

"Get in!" she shouted. "Move!"

So what else could I do? I got in.

Tires squealing, Sabrina pulled out of the parking lot. She drove fast, glancing in the rearview mirror every few seconds.

"Oh, shoot."

I could hear the wail of a police siren. I prayed that it was Deputy Pete who was following us, not that smart Sheriff Dupree.

"Who's driving?" I asked, trying to see behind us.

"I think it's the sheriff," Sabrina said, increasing speed. "Darn!"

"I guess he didn't get confirmation from the FBI," I said.

"Yeah," Sabrina said, wheeling around a corner with another squeal of tires. "Or else he found out this car is stolen."

13//straight for the sun

"Next stop, Arizona," Sabrina said, gunning the motor.

"You stole a *car?*" I shouted. "This is a stolen *car?*"

"You're repeating yourself, Ryan," Sabrina said calmly. "Now, would you mind being quiet? I have to concentrate on my driving. I can pick up the interstate in ten miles."

This seemed like a good suggestion, since we were going close to ninety miles an hour. And the siren's wail was getting louder.

So I sat back and let Sabrina drive. She squealed onto the interstate and moved immediately into the left lane. She kept checking the rearview. "He's gaining."

"I know," I said. "Maybe we should just pull over." I was tired of running, to be honest.

I was ready to give up. How had I ended up in a stolen car in New Mexico?

Sabrina changed lanes again. She checked the rearview mirror. I looked at my side mirror.

"Sabrina, you've got to pull over!" I cried. "He's right on our tail!"

"Hang on," Sabrina said as we zoomed past an exit. Suddenly, she whipped the wheel to the right. We bumped over the curb, then over the grassy median. My teeth rattled as we landed with a jolt back onto the road. Sabrina pressed the accelerator to the floor, and we zoomed down the exit ramp.

"That should slow him down a bit," she said.

We sped down a secondary road. Within a quarter mile, we could hear the siren again.

"No problem," Sabrina said through gritted teeth. She hunched over the wheel, straining to see ahead. I checked the side view, but there was no sign of Sheriff Dupree.

"Hang on!" Sabrina shouted suddenly.

This time, I paid attention. I grabbed the dashboard as Sabrina suddenly swung off the road onto a dirt track. We jounced down the rutted road, driving so fast that my head actually hit the top of the cab.

Then Sabrina made another turn, onto an even smaller dirt track. She finally had to slow down as we bumped over roots and occasionally had to drive through bushes overhanging the road. Then she stopped the car and rolled down the window.

"What—" I started.

"Shhh," she interrupted. She cocked her head, listening for the siren. I could hear it faintly. It rose in volume, then slowly died.

Sabrina grinned. "Let me give you a tip, Ryan. If you ever have to steal a car, get a four-wheel drive."

She put the car in gear again and drove. She drove fast, but not at the breakneck speed she'd used before.

"Okay," I said. "As Spock would say, explain."

Sabrina shot a quick, merry glance at me. "Where should I start?"

"Jump right in anywhere," I said. "Like,

how do you know how to steal a car?"

"I don't," Sabrina said. "The keys were in the ignition. And I figured we'd need the car. Don't worry, Ryan. We can drop it off somewhere and call the guy to tell him where it is. The registration is in the glove compartment."

"How did you get that ID for David Wallaby?" I asked.

Sabrina shrugged. "I'm a teenager. And a teenager knows that in every town, no matter how small, there's someone who can make fake IDs. I told him I needed to get my boyfriend into a bar."

"But David Wallaby?" I asked. "How did you know what name to use?"

"I didn't," Sabrina said, flashing her dynamite grin. "David Wallaby was my boyfriend in second grade. I just came up with the name on the spot. And now, with computers, you can make an ID in whatever name you want. And since I lifted your wallet, I had your driver's license. We just scanned in your photo. Sorry it took so long."

"No problemo," I said, dazed.

"Any more questions?"

"What about the McDoogles?" I asked.

"I told them we'd be delayed a day, and we'd try to hook up with them in Flagstaff," Sabrina explained. "They were freaked out when the cop took you away, so I think they were actually happy to take off. They probably don't care if we show up in Flagstaff at all."

"So what do we do now?" I said.

Sabrina laughed. The window was still down, and the chilly breeze swept her dark hair back from her face. "We drive," she said. She glanced at me. "Come on, Ryan. You're out of danger. We're free. Can't you admit that you're having fun?"

"If this is fun, I'll take boredom any day," I said. But Sabrina was close to being right. I did feel exhilarated to be free, and moving fast, away from danger.

"Grinch," Sabrina said. "Anyway, there's no map in the car, but if we keep heading west, we'll be okay. Straight toward the setting sun."

The sun was an orange ball on the horizon. It streamed into the car. I could feel the cold air, but I felt warm in the pool of sunlight. I didn't know what was behind us, or ahead of us, but I felt ready to take it on, alert and alive.

And that was my last thought before I fell asleep.

It must have been the tension, because I slept soundly, even as the Jeep jolted over the mountain road.

When I woke, the sun was bloodred, hanging over the peaks around us. The sky was streaked purple and orange. We were minutes away from complete darkness, jolting sharply uphill on a road that was only a little wider than a jogging trail.

I yawned and stretched. "Where are we?"

"In the Sangre de Cristo Mountains," Sabrina said. "East of Santa Fe."

I remembered enough from Spanish class to translate. "The Blood of Christ?" I looked out at the ponderosa pines, tinged with red. I shivered. "Shouldn't we find a place to camp tonight?"

"We're almost there," Sabrina said. Her

jaw was set, and she was sitting straight upright, peering ahead.

"Almost *where?*" I asked.

"There's a place up here to stop for the night," Sabrina answered in a voice that told me she was barely listening to me.

"I thought you'd never been to New Mexico," I said. Sabrina didn't answer. Suddenly, something didn't seem right. Sabrina even looked different, erect and tense. Her hands gripped the steering wheel, and her jaw worked back and forth nervously.

She switched on the headlights. They illuminated a high-wire fence ahead. I could just make out the sign:

KEEP OUT

ELECTRIFIED FENCE

BAD DOG

"Guess they don't want company," I said.

Sabrina didn't answer. She stopped the Jeep and got out. She walked to the gate and bent over. I saw her twirl some kind of combination lock. The gate swung open.

Sabrina got back in the car and put it in gear.

"What's going on?" I said. I began to think I was talking to myself. Sabrina didn't even seem to hear me.

She drove through the gate, got out, and locked it again. Then she slipped behind the wheel and drove down the road. I was just wondering how to phrase a question she'd actually answer when I saw lights ahead.

"Where are we?" I blurted.

Finally, she answered. "A place where you'll be safe," she said softly.

She drove up and parked outside a strange rambling structure. Light came from behind curtained windows, and there was one lamp lit outside an iron gate. From the glare of the headlights, I could just make out the strange shadows cast on the walls. I realized that the house was built out of halved automobile tires. The gaps were filled in with cement.

"What is this? Spaceship Goodyear?"

Sabrina switched off the headlights. She reached out and squeezed my knee. "Just let me talk. We might not get a chance to be alone again. Ryan, I really do care for you. Please believe that."

"But, why—"

She squeezed again, and I stopped talking. Her expression was so fierce.

"Trust me," she said. "I did what I thought was best. I—"

Suddenly, floodlights blazed to life. I could see now that the structure was big and rambling, larger than I'd thought. Then I saw, pulled up under a tree, the red pickup.

"The Caravan!" I said. "You brought me to them! Sabrina—"

The harsh light lit her eyes, making them look the color of ice on a lake. She just stared at me, no expression in her eyes.

A tall, lanky man emerged from behind the high wall surrounding the compound. He had silver hair and was dressed in black jeans and a blue denim shirt. He walked toward the Jeep and opened the driver's door.

"I was worried. The police scanner said—"

"It's okay," Sabrina said. "We made it."

The man's eyes were the palest, palest blue, bleached denim with a silvery cast. Like Sabrina's eyes.

She got out and stood next to him. "Now, say hello, Dad," she said.

He smiled. "Hello, Jeremy," he said. "Welcome home."

My mouth closed and opened, fishlike.

Jeremy?

"How was your trip?" the tall man asked.

"A few bumps along the way," Sabrina—Jeremy!—answered. "But basically okay."

He squeezed her shoulders. "You done good, kiddo."

I gazed at the two of them in disbelief. They were so calm. So . . . normal. As though Sabrina had just returned from an outing at Ye Olde Malt Shoppe on Main Street, U.S.A. Instead of racing through New Mexico on the run from the cops, and betraying me along the way.

The tall man looked over Sabrina's shoulder at me. "You must be Ryan. Welcome."

"Ryan, this is my father," Sabrina said.

"Wait, don't tell me," I said. "Let me guess, because this is really fun. GuildMaster."

The man gazed at me calmly and politely. He was even smiling. I wanted to punch him.

"You can call me Cole, if you prefer," he said.

"Actually, I have a few other names reserved," I said. "Like kidnapper."

He didn't flinch. "Don't judge until you hear our story," he said pleasantly. "Now, you're both probably hungry and cold. Come inside."

I wanted to refuse. I wanted to cross my arms and stay in the car. I wanted to wrench the keys from Sabrina's hand and peel out of there.

But how would I get past that gate? And where would I go if I could? I was in the middle of nowhere. They knew the territory. They would find me.

I looked at Sabrina. I *willed* her to look back. But she stared at her shoes.

I didn't feel like exploding. I felt like *imploding*. I wished my whole body would compress, would blow inward, would turn into particles of dust that would be carried away by the wind. I would orbit the earth for centuries. I would contribute to the greenhouse effect. I would refract light; I would cause spectacular sunsets.

I would no longer have a body.

I would no longer have a heart.

But I didn't implode. So I followed them inside.

We walked into a long open room with tables lining the walls. The tables were piled with computer equipment. Some of it was piled on the floor. Wires and cables snaked along the floor. There was no other furniture except for a long bench in front of one of those triangular fireplaces they use in the Southwest. I could smell wood burning.

I checked out the computer equipment. It looked serious. I ticked off the hardware in my head. Very impressive. State of the art.

Two people worked in a far corner. I could see the blue glow of the screens.

"Our main workroom site," Cole said. "This way."

We walked through a low doorway into

a narrow corridor. The walls were made of the same tire and cement mixture. Then we emerged into another large room. This one was filled with three long tables. Chairs lined up along each table. It looked like a school or office cafeteria.

At one end of the room, I could see the open kitchen. Two people were in there, chopping and cooking. Several people sat at the far table, eating from colorful plates. Something was odd about the scene, and I realized what it was. First of all, everyone was wearing black jeans and blue denim shirts. Second, no one was talking, or even making a sound. Even the chopping in the kitchen was quiet.

"This is quad B," Cole said. "Dining, laundry, showers."

"Fascinating," I said.

Cole pulled out seats for me and . . . Jeremy. She was no longer Sabrina, the girl I knew who grinned and made jokes, the photographer who I realized now didn't even carry a camera, the girl who had held me and said, *I'll help you.*

She had morphed into a new creature

called Jeremy. I had to reformat everything I knew about her.

Cole motioned to the woman in the kitchen, and she nodded. A moment later, two plates were placed in front of Jeremy and me, along with a pitcher of water and glasses.

"Vegetable enchiladas and black beans," Cole said.

The smell was incredible. The cheese bubbled on top, and the black beans were studded with onions and herbs. I actually felt hungry. Jeremy picked up her fork and dug right in, but I hesitated.

"Eat," Cole told me. "Sona is a good cook. She was a lousy programmer. So now she just works in the kitchen."

I didn't pick up my fork.

Cole shrugged. "Whatever pleases you."

"What would please me is to go home," I said.

"But you can't go home, can you, Ryan?" Cole asked. "And, anyway, we don't go down the mountain after dark. So relax. I assure you, we're not keeping you against your will."

"Are you serious?" I said. "You just framed me, kidnapped me, and lied to me. I'm somewhere I don't want to be, behind a locked gate, with no way out. And I'm not being held against my will?"

"We'll take you down the mountain in daylight," Cole answered. "Ryan, you can leave when you want. We just wanted to talk to you. We wanted you to hear the truth. Because you are one of us, even if you don't realize it. Your mind doesn't work in the old way. I guarantee that you'll agree with what you'll see here. You'll realize that we're not criminals. I even hope that you choose to join us."

"Don't hold your breath," I said. I didn't believe a word he said. The place gave me the creeps, and I didn't believe I'd be able to leave whenever I wanted. They'd brainwash me, and soon I'd be wearing a denim shirt and black jeans and not even clinking my silverware when I ate.

"If you're not doing anything illegal, why are you hiding out here in Spaceship Goodyear?" I asked angrily. "Why did you kidnap me? I want out of here, now!"

"I told you," Cole said, lowering his voice, "we never go down the mountain after dark—"

I pushed back my chair. It slid backward and crashed into the table behind me. Everyone looked up from their meal, but quickly looked down again. Jeremy's fork poised in midair. She half-rose, but quickly sat down again when Cole made a gesture.

"Maybe you should change the policy," I said loudly. "The Jeep has lights, doesn't it? You can make it down. Or I'll drive it down myself and take my chances. If I'm not a prisoner, give me the keys!"

"Ryan, calm down. We're not—"

"People know where I am, you know," I said. "The McDoogles will be suspicious if Sabrina and I don't meet them in Flagstaff. They'll ask questions. And that sheriff was smart—he'll figure out who I am. And then he'll figure out who Sabrina is, too. Excuse me—*Jeremy.*"

Cole gave a sad smile and shook his head. And just then, I heard someone singing behind me. It was the theme from the old *Mary Tyler Moore* show.

"... *who can take a nothing day, and suddenly make it all seem worthwhile* ..."

I whirled around. Behind me, Bud and Twyla were in the kitchen. Twyla was tasting something in a big pot, and Bud was filling a plate with enchiladas.

My stomach seemed to drop into my shoes. Bud grinned. He waved his fork at me. "Hey, little buddy! Glad you finally made it!"

I blinked, hard, as hopelessness and rage swept over me. Bud and Twyla blurred in front of my eyes. I was deep into a nightmare I couldn't escape.

Because now I realized that nobody in the world knew where I was. And there was nobody to rescue me.

15//the emperor has no clothes

I'd been taken in. Duped from the jump.

Me, the person who didn't trust anyone. What a joke I was.

"Sit down, Ryan," Cole said quietly. "This isn't a cult, okay? All I'm asking for is a morning. One morning. Tomorrow I'll give you the tour. And if you want to leave in the afternoon, you can. You have my word."

I didn't know whether to believe him or not. But it didn't matter much. I didn't have a choice. I was staying here until he wanted to let me go.

"Look, maybe our methods were a little heavy-handed," Cole said. "But we didn't mean to harm you. We'd never let you get caught by the FBI. We needed you to go on the run. We needed you here."

"But why?" I burst out. "Why me?"

"You'll find out tomorrow," Cole said. "Right now, I think you should eat. And get a good night's sleep."

They brought me to a chamber that was more like a cell. But it had a tiny fireplace, and it was warm. A futon was rolled out on a platform, and there was a thick quilt folded on top.

"Here is your cube," Cole said. "Just the basics, I'm afraid. But you'll be comfortable."

"Sleep well," Jeremy said. It was the first sentence she'd directed at me since I'd arrived.

"Oh, I'm sure I'll sleep like a baby," I said sarcastically. Jeremy didn't look at me.

"Jeremy told me that you two became friends on the road," Cole said to me.

"We're not friends," I said scornfully. "You can't be friends with a person impersonator. She's a fake. She only resembles the real thing. She morphed into cheese food."

Jeremy swung her head away so that her long hair hid her face.

"Perhaps you'd better say good night, Jeremy," Cole said with a sigh.

Jeremy didn't say a word. She just seemed to melt away through the doorway.

Good riddance, I thought.

"You hurt her feelings," Cole told me. "She acted from the heart, Ryan. But I won't interfere between the two of you. Good night."

It was late, and I was tired. Exhausted, in fact. I could barely make it back to my futon. I fell asleep immediately. My last thought was the way Jeremy had looked when she'd said *trust me* in the car.

Trust me . . .

"That was my first mistake," I said, and fell asleep.

In the morning, I headed toward the dining area. Everyone looked busy and purposeful. They smiled at me when they passed, or nodded in a friendly way.

In the daylight, the place looked less mysterious. There weren't cobwebs hanging from the rafters, and no one gave me an evil glare. If this was a cult, it didn't seem sinister.

Sunlight poured through the windows, and people didn't go around with gooney smiles on their faces, or hand me plastic flowers. As a matter of fact, the compound just seemed like a giant office.

The dining area was empty, so I sat at a table alone. In just a few seconds, Sona appeared. She said good morning and placed a bowl of steaming oatmeal in front of me, along with a plate of sliced apples and raisins. Then she poured me a cup of tea in a thick mug with bright blue and yellow stripes outlined in black.

I was starving, so I ate every bite. Sona reappeared to refill my bowl. This time, she added a plate of thickly sliced cinnamon toast. It tasted like the best meal I'd ever had.

"This is great. It makes me sorry I passed up your enchiladas," I said.

She smiled. "Just don't miss my chicken stew tonight."

"Sorry," I said. "I'm heading out later this morning."

The smile faded, and she bent over to refill my mug. "When you're done, Cole will be waiting in quad A—that's where you came in last night—at site 2. The doors are numbered."

"Like my days," I said gloomily.

Sona didn't smile, or comment. She faded back into the kitchen.

I gulped more tea, then headed off to meet Cole.

But I decided to shake things up a bit. Sona was busy in the kitchen, so instead of heading back to quad A, I followed a different corridor. I could always say I'd gotten lost. It would be easy, because the narrow corridors snaked around confusingly.

I turned left after I passed the showers, going toward the rear of the building. I passed a laundry area. The corridor branched off, and I went left.

Behind a door, I heard an odd, humming noise, and I stopped. I pushed it open and peeked in.

Jeremy was bent over a pottery wheel. I watched as she controlled it with her feet. She was making a bowl out of clay, and she looked pretty expert at it. No wonder she had such strong hands. She frowned as she smoothed the sides of the bowl.

Shelves lined the walls, filled with plates and cups striped in that same bright blue and yellow pattern.

"This must be your darkroom," I said.

Jeremy flinched, but she didn't look up.

"I bet you can't even load a Polaroid," I said.

Jeremy stopped the wheel abruptly. The bowl collapsed in on itself. "What is it, Ryan? Do you have something to say?"

"What else did you lie about?" I asked. "Eric Clapton? Bad science fiction movies? I bet you hate Cheerios, don't you?"

Jeremy swung her ponytail behind her shoulder. "Yes!" she shouted. "I lied about all those things, okay? Is that what you want to hear? We looked up your video records and tracked the hits you made on the Web. We found out what you liked, so that you'd think you'd found a soul mate! Okay?"

"Yeah, cheese food," I said disgustedly. "That's what I wanted to hear. I wanted to hear what a lying traitor you really are, right from your own lying lips."

Jeremy smacked the clay with her fist.

"Okay, you've heard it, Ryan," she said. "I lied, because I had to. My mission was to get you here—"

"And you chose to accept it," I said. "No matter what you had to do, right?"

Her pale eyes fixed on me. "That's right. No matter what I had to do. But I didn't lie about important stuff. I didn't lie when I said I liked you and cared about you."

"And I'm supposed to *believe* you?" I said with a strange, choked laugh. "Do you think I'm stupid, or just dumb?"

Jeremy looked down. She kneaded the clay for a minute.

"I think you're fantastic," she said softly. "I think you're the smartest guy I ever met, and the funniest, and the nicest."

I pushed off the door frame. "Whoa. I'm so flattered. Considering that your pool of candidates here is so large."

"We didn't always live at the Compound, Ryan," Jeremy said. "I didn't lie about moving around a lot. That's why we bonded like we did. I went to a zillion different schools, too."

She went back to working the clay. "My

father isn't a bad person. He's a tad on the obsessive side—"

"That's putting it lightly—"

"—but he believes in what he's doing. We're the good guys. Dad sees a better world in the new millennium."

"Right," I said. "Just don't pass me the Kool-Aid."

"Aren't you supposed to meet him this morning?" Jeremy asked.

"Yeah. He's giving me the free tour of FantasyLand."

She sighed. "Then why don't you meet him, and find out about us. Then we can talk."

"I have no interest in talking to cheese food," I said. My face was hot, and I was shaking. I stalked out, slamming the door behind me.

Cole was standing in the hallway, his arms crossed. If he had heard my conversation with Jeremy, he gave no sign.

"Lead on, o fearless Guild Master Leader Führer," I said. "I'm ready for the tour."

Cole led me through the Compound,

concentrating on the work sites. I tried not to show how impressed I was with the amount of hardware and the kind of work they were doing. If this were a university, I'd sign up.

We finally stopped in the biggest site in quad A. It was a large, windowless room filled with computer equipment. There were no dividers between the desks, and a cork-lined wall on one side was studded with fluttering pages and Post-it notes. Monitors, coding manuals, cables, wires, and circuit boards were everywhere. On a dry-erase board was boldly written: WHEN IT'S DEAD SOLID PERFECT, CHECK IT AGAIN. TWICE.

Two workers were playing Nerf darts. I noticed how they didn't quickly start working when they saw Cole. They just waved their darts at him in a friendly way.

So the guy wasn't a slave driver. But that didn't mean he was a prince.

"You know, Ryan, better than most, that our future as a civilization resides in bits," Cole told me. "Coded information that flies through cables that are hooked into systems. But how many people have asked this question: How vulnerable are we to the system as a whole? What if one entity got hold of all that information that's held in computers all over the country?"

"One group can't," I said. "That's what passwords and gates are for. We have privacy controls."

"Which any reasonably savvy high school student can get past," Cole said. "If *you* can get root access to an online service, or shut down an electrical system, what do you think one group of geniuses could do? What do you think the government could do, or the bankers, or a foreign country?"

"Or the Millennium Caravan?" I asked.

He shook his head. "On the contrary. We are here to ensure that democracy stays alive."

"That sounds pretty intense," I said. "Like you're Super Cop of the Net."

Then I noticed the guy sitting at the terminal nearest me. It was the driver of the red pickup. The guy with the hair like wire cables who'd been cutting the lawn in brown shoes.

"I think you've met Komodo," Cole said.

"We go by online addresses here."

"Hi, Catcher," Komodo said.

"Hey," I said. "Let me give you a piece of advice. Next time you go on surveillance, buy yourself a pair of sneakers. Nobody cuts a lawn in brown shoes."

Cole shook his head. "Komodo is our encryption expert. Surveillance is not his bag. Actually, we're all amateurs at this spy stuff."

"I wouldn't say that," I said. "Your daughter was a real pro. She can lie like a lawyer."

"And this is Topcat," Cole said, introducing me to a guy in oversized glasses who gave me a jerky nod and turned back to his monitor. "And NancE."

A thin, nervous woman with orange hair gave me a quick smile.

"You should be flattered that we chose you, Ryan," he said. "Our group is filled with only the best computer minds in the country. We have original COBOL coders. Some of these folks have worked for the government. They held positions with top-level access."

"Okay, I'm impressed," I said. "But you still haven't spelled out what all this brain activity is for."

"Good point. Let's sit down." Cole waved me to a low bench.

"The reason I mention how important these people are is to show you how crucial you are, Ryan. You were our number one choice for the draft here."

"The *draft?* That's a polite way to refer to a kidnapping," I said. "Did you frame all of these guys with the FBI, too?"

Cole shook his head. "They're all here because they want to be. We contacted them over the Net, and they came. You're the only one we've had to use ... extraordinary measures to get to come here."

"Okay," I said. "I'm still asking the same question. Why?"

"Do you know the story of the emperor who had no clothes?" Cole asked me.

"Sure," I said. "I read it when I was a kid. This tailor pretended to have made this cool suit, only it didn't really exist. So he fooled the emperor by raving about it, so the emperor pretended he could see it, too.

Then all the people pretended he was a styling dude, because they were afraid to mention he was in his boxers."

"Exactly," Cole said. "Well, our computer age is that emperor. The entire structure of our system is hanging by an invisible thread. Everyone knows it's there, but they won't admit how much trouble we're in. But when the millennium comes, when the clock ticks over to one minute after midnight on December 31, 1999, all the rules will change, my friend."

"The Millennium Virus," I agreed with a shrug. "Most computer software—especially the old computer languages like COBOL and FORTRAN, which are still embedded in lots of systems—format the date in six digits and employ a two-digit shorthand. Which means that calendars will spin back to 1900, and everything will get snarled. But—"

"Everything," Cole interrupted, "from banking to ballistic missiles. From your e-mail to your phone service to your tax return. High-speed elevators and traffic lights and air traffic control—"

"I have news for you." This time, I interrupted him. I could tell he didn't like it, but he concealed his irritation under his usual half smile. "Everybody knows about it. And hundreds of people are working on the problem. I know there's a whole doom and gloom scenario, but everyone from the Feds to the phone company is overhauling their mainframes. There's this company called SysTem2000 that's practically cornered the market on recoding."

Cole nodded. "I see you keep up with cyber news. SysTem2000 has government contracts, banking contracts, communications contracts . . . they are the most knowledgeable, the quickest, the smartest. The projected numbers for what the 2000 conversion will cost are staggering. The IRS alone estimates $155 million. The Pentagon won't release a number, but it's got to be more. The biggest banking chain in the U.S. estimates $250 to 300 million."

"So what's your point?" I asked. "If coders will take care of most of the problems, the emperor seems pretty well dressed, to me. Nothing's going to crash."

"We'll just have to see, won't we," Cole answered.

"Yeah, sure," I said. "Remind me to call you on January second in the year 2000. Can I go now?"

But something wasn't right. I knew that Cole was leaving something out. He looked confident, almost smug. And he still hadn't answered my question. Why did he have COBOL coders, and hackers, and systems experts all working here? And what did he want with me?

And then a Roman candle shot off in my brain, and I got it. "Hold the phone," I said slowly. "You're not going to wait and see, are you." I looked at Cole dead-on. "*You're* SysTem2000."

Cole's smile broadened.

I felt my breath leave me in a *whoosh*. "That means that *you'll* be the one in control. Of just about everything."

16//phreaked out

Cole beamed at me. "You see why we chose you?" he said. His pale blue eyes twinkled in an admiring way that made me feel like an Einstein genius. "You're one of us. You're intuitive. You can make the leaps. I knew I was right about you."

For a minute, I felt pleased, as though I had just been admitted into some elite fraternity. Then I remembered that I thought fraternities were bogus.

"Don't look so nervous, Ryan," Cole said, still smiling. "Everything we do here is perfectly legal. SysTem2000 is recoding systems for corporations and government services all over the country. But in our codes, we're leaving something behind."

"A virus," I guessed.

"We prefer to think of it as a beep," Cole

corrected. "A warning beep. On the stroke of midnight, January 1, 2000, all the controlling systems of the United States—financial, commercial, communications, transportation—will be in the hands of SysTem2000. Which is actually, of course, the operative branch of the Millennium Caravan."

I tried not to gulp. "And what will you do then?"

Cole smiled. "Absolutely nothing. That's the beauty of the plan. That's why it's not illegal. It will be enough to *have* the power. Then we'll get on the communication network and inform the government and the businesses that we have it. People will know how vulnerable they are to control. There will be a revolution in people's minds. They will realize that they are slaves to technology. They will realize how wrong they were to rely on technology so completely. And then, at last, they will be ready for the new millennium. Because they will go back. To a simpler age, a more decentralized infrastructure. They will realize that the basis of survival depends on *com-*

munity. A community where people see each other, know each other, are in each other's living rooms and courtrooms and offices. Atomic particles are the basis of life, Ryan. Not bits that travel through cables! That's just air!"

Cole's eyes were shining. His voice was low and thrilling. His words pounded in my head, and everything sounded logical and right. Was he a kook—or a genius?

"That's why we call ourselves a caravan, Ryan. I don't know if you remember your history, but back in the Middle Ages, groups of traveling merchants with the same interests formed caravans for protection. They stood by each other in case of attack, and looked out for each other's interests. These caravans became guilds. Brother protected brother. Worker protected worker. Guilds formed alliances with other guilds. It was a much more democratic system. We can return to it. We have to go smaller, not bigger. We have to decentralize, not centralize. We will have a philosophical revolution for the new millennium. A peaceful revolution. And this small group of visionaries shall lead the way."

Cole gestured to the people on the computers, playing Nerf darts, drinking tea.

What was wrong with this picture? I tried to picture the geeky guy holding a Nerf dart striding into a revolution.

"Join us, Ryan," Cole said. "Don't you want to save the world?"

"You seem to have everything figured out already," I said. "What do you need me for?"

Cole turned to me. He leaned closer. "The national power grid, first of all. We haven't cracked it. We're going to have to hack our way in. It's the last piece of the puzzle. And we need you."

So that was it! I almost laughed out loud. They'd chased me, framed me, tried to recruit me—all for something I didn't know how to do!

"Sorry to disappoint you," I said. "I already told Sab—Jeremy. I *can't* crack the grid. I exaggerated, and the newspaper got the story wrong."

"I know that," Cole said. "But that doesn't

mean you can't crack it if you try again. But this time, you'll have people working for you, and better equipment. Can you imagine it, Ryan? I'll put a whole team at your disposal."

"Sorry," I said. "You made your pitch, and I'm not interested. Now, when can I leave?"

He waited a moment. Then he stood. "All right. I won't try to change your mind."

He walked to a phone and punched out a few numbers. "LuddMan, bring the truck around. I need you to drive to Santa"—He stopped and listened. I saw his lips tighten— "I didn't give authorization for"—He stopped again—"I see." I could see his muscles working as he tried to control himself. It seemed real, not faked.

I had a feeling I wasn't getting down the mountain just yet.

Cole hung up. "This is embarrassing. Considering my promise to you. But apparently, Bud took the pickup down the mountain for supplies." He pushed his hand through his cropped silver hair. "Things aren't too organized around here," he said. Then he grinned at me. "That should prove we're not a cult. Tomorrow, someone will drive you to Santa Fe or Albuquerque. I'll even throw in bus fare to California."

"What about the Jeep?" I asked.

"I didn't want you to have to ride in a stolen car," he said. "And nobody wanted it on the premises. We drove it down the mountain early this morning."

"So much for your promises," I said. My heart was beating fast. I felt trapped.

He flashed a grin that reminded me of Sabrina/Jeremy's. It was lopsided, and you caught a flash of mischief that made you want to be friends forever. I fought against the feeling.

"Well, I guess you get a day off," he said. "Bud is usually gone all day. Doesn't get back until dusk."

"First thing tomorrow, though?" I asked.

Cole nodded. His gaze was clear, sincere. "You have my word."

I had lunch with NancE and someone called Hypertex, whom everyone called

Tex. We chatted about tech stuff, and I actually enjoyed myself. They didn't seem like zombies, or weirdos. They seemed perfectly normal, aside from being geeks. NancE had this way of twitching her nose every few seconds, but I felt it was a tic, not a symptom of psychosis. And Tex's ability to construct a castle out of tea bags seemed playful, not sinister.

After lunch, NancE showed me to the back of the compound. She pointed to a trail that cut sharply up the hill that rose in back of a storage shed.

"That's a nice walk," she said. "There's a view at the top."

I knew that the trail would only take me to the perimeter and back again. But if there was some sort of overlook, I might get a better sense of where I was.

I started hiking. The smell of pine and what NancE told me was piñon trees was fresh and pungent. The sun felt good on my shoulders.

When the trail turned a corner of the hill, I saw Jeremy sitting on a grassy knoll, her knees tucked up under her chin.

I could have kept on walking. But I figured that as long as I was here for another day, I might as well talk to her. I walked closer.

"So when we were chatting online when this all started, why did you keep calling me 'dude' and 'my man'?" I asked.

She shielded her eyes with her hand so she could look up at me. "I was trying to sound like a guy. Lame, huh?"

"Totally," I said. I sat down next to her.

"Your father has some wacked-out ideas," I said. "We're all supposed to go back to the Middle Ages in the year 2000."

Jeremy shrugged. "Do you think civilization is going along so great? Do you think we're really thinking about what we're doing, putting our very existence into machines?"

"Computers don't control us, Jeremy," I said. "We program them."

"And then they beat us at chess," Jeremy answered. "Look, that's Dad's point. Computers can do what we tell them to. But what happens if one person, or one institution, controls them?"

"I've been talking to your father all morning," I said, sighing. "Spare me the lecture, will you? This place gives me a headache." I flopped back on the grass.

Jeremy gave a low laugh. "I know what you mean. It gets to you sometimes." She stared down at her hands on her knees.

"Look," she said. "Back in the eighties, hackers were the ones who forced the banks and the phone company and the government to take security seriously. They showed people how vulnerable their privacy was. And encryption software and privacy codes were developed. We're planning the same thing, except we're being organized about it. It's a giant wake-up call. But what comes after will benefit everyone."

"But it's *illegal*," I pointed out.

"So is what you did at your school, technically," Jeremy said. "But you didn't think you deserved to go to jail, did you?"

"But that was a prank!" I exclaimed. "It's not the same thing at all."

Jeremy flopped back on the grass. She turned to face me, leaning on her elbow.

Her face was full of mischief. It was a face I'd missed.

"Of course it is," she said. "Don't you get it, Ryan? This is the biggest prank in the history of the world. Don't you want to be part of it?"

The next morning, Cole came to my cube before breakfast.

"I have bad news," he told me. "Bud called last night. The truck blew a rod. He'll have to stay in Santa Fe for several days until they order the part and fix it."

"Do you really expect me to believe that?" I said.

"Ryan, I can't convince you, so why should I try?" Cole asked. "I'm trying to arrange other transportation for you. Until then—"

"What?" I asked.

"You don't seem to be having a terrible time," Cole said. "Are you? I saw you playing chess with Jeremy last night."

She'd challenged me after dinner. We'd sat by the fire in a back "lounging room" in quad D, where most of the sleeping cubes were. The light had been low, and the room was quiet, even though about four other people were there reading, or doing cross-word puzzles. I'd watched Jeremy's long, tan fingers on the chess pieces, and the flicker of firelight on her skin. I'd had trouble with my concentration.

"Didn't you enjoy it?" Cole asked.

"No," I said. "I lost. So do you think I'll be out of here by Christmas?"

"Ryan, we're in an isolated part of the mountains," Cole said. He finally sounded exasperated, which reassured me. He sounded like a normal person. I was used to how people sounded when I got on their nerves. "We rely on one piece of transportation that breaks down every now and again. I can't manufacture a new car just for you. Can't you just hang here for another day or two?"

"I don't have a choice, do I?" I countered.

"No, I guess you don't," Cole said.

I hoped I looked angry, and put out. It would serve him right. But I didn't feel that way.

I thought back on the way Jeremy's skin had glowed in the firelight. Once, her fingers had brushed mine as she'd moved a piece.

So I admit it—part of me was happy. I would have more time with Jeremy.

17//just about perfect

Jeremy and I passed the days talking, eating, and hiking. Cole gave Jeremy a few days off so she could spend more time with me. She even taught me how to work with clay. I made the most lopsided cup you've ever seen.

The two days passed quicker than I could have imagined. The one thing that was nagging at me was that my mom might be worried.

"I'd like to send her an e-mail," I told Jeremy. "Just to let her know I'm okay."

"You'll have to ask Cole," Jeremy told me. "All outgoing mail goes through him, for security reasons. We just have internal e-mail. I'm sure he'll let you do it." Then, she looked guilty. "Actually," she said in a low voice, "I cracked his code. I had this boyfriend from where we lived before, and I didn't want my dad reading my mail. He never knew."

"So you could send a message to my mom," I said.

Jeremy looked uneasy. "I think you'd better go through Dad," she said. "We're on this super security alert."

Something *pinged* when she said that. It made me uneasy. But I went to Cole and asked if I could send an e-mail. To my surprise, he agreed right away. He just requested that I not reveal my whereabouts. Since I was using his mail service, I had to obey. But even if I could manage to sneak in some secret code telling her I was in the mountains outside Santa Fe, what could Mom do, anyway?

Besides, in less than twenty-four hours, I'd be in Santa Fe, boarding a bus for California.

That night, I climbed into bed. Tomorrow Bud would be back. I could leave in the late afternoon, Cole said. After lunch.

I felt restless and wide awake. There was no window, so I had to imagine a dark night, and a silver moon. I felt so confused.

All I had wanted to do was get away. And now, all I could think of was how to come up with more than one reason to stay. I couldn't stay for a girl. I had to believe in what Cole was doing.

What was waiting for me out there? College would just be High School, Part Two. I had connected with Jeremy, but that didn't mean I would ever be able to connect with another girl I liked so much. And Mom was way back in North Carolina. I had no other family. No other friends.

Then I thought about the days I'd spent here. I thought about how everyone was working on something that fascinated me. How the surroundings were so pleasant. How the landscape was so beautiful. Why go to college and study World History 101 when I could make history right here?

Here was a place where people talked about the same things that interested me. In his spare time, Komodo was designing a computer game. NancE was fascinated by digital manipulation of images. She was the one who'd given Jeremy a crash course in digital photography.

Something pricked at me, some quiet unease. I was getting sleepy, and I tried to chase the thought. My mind was getting lazy, spiraling toward sleep.

And then I got it. *Nobody laughed here.*

Everybody smiled. Everyone was pleasant. But I'd yet to hear one good laugh.

I turned over. In the gloom, I could just make out that my door was opening. Jeremy slipped inside. She was dressed in sweatpants and a white T-shirt. She padded toward me. Her hair was jet black, and her eyes looked like chips of starlight.

She stretched out on the bed, her head by my feet, her feet by my head.

"I couldn't sleep," she said.

"Me, either," I said. I pulled the blanket so that it was half over her, and half over me.

"I wish you wouldn't go," she said softly. Her hand found mine. Warmth seemed to flow from her fingers into mine, up my veins, pulsing up toward my chest. It hit my heart.

"Imagine if you stayed," she whispered. "We could be together all the time.

Wouldn't that be just about perfect?"

I swallowed. "Yeah."

"We could have what we talked about right here," Jeremy said. "Remember? We could be together, in the same place. Studying and working and goofing off."

Her sigh floated up toward me, a soft breath in the darkness. "Don't say anything. I know you won't stay. Can't. It's just that . . . I'm so lonesome, Ryan. And I'll miss you so much."

Jeremy's voice sounded choked. I pictured the tears on her cheeks. I felt myself melt. I felt myself fall. All I wanted at that moment was to say yes. *I'll stay, Jeremy. I'll stay for you.*

I came a hair close to saying it. But I thought about the silent dining room, the quiet smiles. I still felt there was something creepy about this place.

So I squeezed her fingers and let them go. "Let's get some sleep," I said. "Good night, Jeremy."

She sounded disappointed. "Good night."

##

When I woke up in the morning, Jeremy was gone. I wandered out to the dining hall. It was empty, as usual. No matter how early I woke up, I never beat anybody to breakfast. Actually, most of the Caravan members ate breakfast and then went to sleep. Many of them worked at night.

Sona had made pancakes. I scarfed down a couple of platefuls.

"Any news on the truck?" I asked Sona.

"After lunch," she said. Sona was not the talkative type.

I went off in search of Jeremy. I checked the studio first, but it was empty. I pushed open the back door and started down the path. The sun was already warm in a bright clear sky as I climbed the hill to the knoll. Jeremy wasn't around. I realized that I'd never kept climbing in search of that panoramic view. Jeremy always stopped here, saying it was her favorite place to sit. This time, I kept going.

The trail twisted sharply uphill. Surrounded by trees, I couldn't make out where I was. I figured I'd reach a fence sooner or later.

Through the trees, I caught a glint of silver. And then I heard the sound of rushing water. A stream. I struck off the trail and slid down over the wet leaves toward the water. I was a city boy. I was a sucker for mountain streams.

It was cool and fast, burbling over the pebbles. I splashed the ice-cold water on my neck, gasping at the shock. This would be a great place to take Jeremy.

I hiked down the creek bed, keeping the trail in sight. Mom and I usually had picked cities to live in. Hiking was a new experience. Once, we'd camped in the Blue Ridge Mountains, when I was about ten. I'd never forgotten how sharp everything looked, as if every branch and leaf had been outlined with a fine ink pen. And I'd seen more birds in a morning than I'd ever noticed before in my life.

I saw a flash of red through the trees. Was it a bird? I left the creek and pushed through the trees. There was no trail here, so I had to jump over branches and logs.

It wasn't a bird. It was a truck, covered in a brown tarp, over which pine branches and leaves had been laid.

It was the red pickup.

18//big lies, little lies

I peeled back part of the tarp. Sure enough, it was the pickup that was supposed to have thrown a rod. The pickup that wouldn't be back until late this afternoon.

A pair of shovels were thrown in the back of the truck. They were caked with red mud. A pair of coveralls and boots were thrown next to them. I saw something white pushed up against the side of the truck and I fished it out. It was a card with a magnetic stripe, like a credit card. But there was no name or account number on it. I stuck it in the pocket of my jeans.

Bud had been gardening, or repairing fences. He'd never gone to Santa Fe at all.

Cole had lied.

Maybe I'd always known it. I mean, I'd definitely suspected it. But I hadn't cared.

What was happening to me?

Is this what brainwashing is like? Does it start slowly, like this? At first, do you think, *I'm not buying this bull.* And then, slowly, as you eat with people and smile at them and have long talks, do you start to slide? Do you start to think, *Maybe this isn't so crazy, after all.*

Maybe this is where I belong.

Because they need me. And nobody ever needed me before. Not like this.

I punched the metal of the truck. My fist sang with the pain of it. I cradled it against me. The pain was mine. The fist was mine. I even liked having the pain. It brought me back to myself.

Sweat broke out on my forehead. I sank to the dirt, still holding my hand. I smelled the piñon trees and the dead leaves, and listened to the stream rushing yards away. I felt every sound, smelled every smell. Because I was reminding myself that I was still here. They hadn't gotten me.

I was still me.

Not that *me* was such a bargain. But it was all I had.

##

I sat on the forest floor, trying to figure out what to do. Cole was keeping me against my will. Did that mean he would keep on doing it? Was I a total prisoner?

Maybe it was time to take a long walk.

I would hike back down the road to the high gate, and find a way around it somehow. Maybe Cole had lied about how isolated the compound was. Maybe there was a ski area nearby, or another house. I would have to take my chances.

I looked up at the sky. There were hours of daylight left. But I should do this the smart way. I should return to the compound and make an excuse. I should say I had a headache and wanted to nap. Jeremy was probably looking for me already.

Jeremy.

Did she know about the truck?

Maybe she didn't know her father was keeping me here, lying to me. Or maybe she did. Maybe Cole had sent her to me last night.

My heart still felt the impact of her. But I forced my brain to work. Sheer stubbornness kick-started it to life because I had a feeling that Cole didn't want it to work. He didn't want me to think. He wanted me to feel.

Would he really use his daughter that way? Was he that low? That manipulative? That . . . *desperate?*

I looked over at the red pickup. Maybe.

Then, I heard a voice calling me. Jeremy.

I quickly moved through the forest until I could see the ridge above me. Keeping behind a tree, I watched her. She was walking slowly, calling my name, and occasionally stopping to wait to hear an answer.

I watched until she stopped. The slope of her shoulders told me she was disappointed. I waited five minutes after she disappeared, and headed back to the compound.

I had barely returned when Topcat told me that Cole wanted to see me in his site. He led me there, then retreated.

Cole whirled around on his chair. "Before Bud gets back," he said, "I wanted to make you a proposition."

I tried to keep my face as neutral as his. "I'm listening."

"Everyone here is a member of the Caravan," Cole began, leaning against his desk. "But what you don't see here is that we have auxiliary members. Members who prefer to stay at their homes and jobs, but who believe in our cause and help us in various ways. One of these members is a nineteen-year-old computer whiz. He completed high school at fifteen, got a job coding in Seattle at sixteen, rose through the ranks, and then invented privacy software so tight that he locked Bill Gates out of his own e-mail. His specialty is encryption codes. Now, the federal government has hired him to work on the power grid access codes in order to make them invincible."

"I see," I said. But I didn't. What did this have to do with me?

Cole crossed his arms. "Naturally, we want the same access. And we want to plant our wake-up call."

"So why do you need me, if you have this whiz kid?"

"David is not willing to do it," Cole said. He shrugged. "He has plans of his own."

"Sounds like a smart guy."

"He lacks commitment," Cole said. "Vision. It's unfortunate. You, however, do not."

I waited.

"What David has agreed to do is disappear for a few weeks," Cole said. "We're sending him on an all-expense-paid trip to Thailand. He's got a thing for Thai food."

"Very generous," I said. "Why?"

"So that someone else can take his place. Later, David can claim he was out of the country and knew nothing about it. If we get caught. But we won't. He has a six-week gig designing and installing encryption software. He'll have access to all privacy controls and passwords. We want them." Cole looked at me and waited.

"Hold it," I said. "You want me to impersonate this guy? Have you forgotten a tiny detail? I'm wanted by the FBI."

"Not anymore," Cole said. "We've erased your file. You're David's height and build, and you look nineteen. And you certainly have his knowledge. We can bring you up to speed here on encryption coding. If you can get the passwords in a day, you won't have to go back. We'll find a doctor who will say you have mono, or some kind of infection, so that it all looks normal—"

"You've already planned this out?"

"We have an ID in the name of David Wallaby for you."

"David Wallaby? Jeremy's first-grade boyfriend?"

Cole smiled. "That was quick thinking on her part. When the cop took you in, she just used the ID we'd already made up for you. We drove it down the mountain to her. That's why it took so long for her to get to you."

So Jeremy had lied about who David Wallaby was, too. Big lies, little lies. For some reason, the little ones stung the most.

"There are compensations for this job, Ryan," Cole said. "Monetary ones. David's fee is substantial. There's a kill clause, but he still gets several thousand. And the Caravan will throw in a bonus. Call it hazard duty, if you like."

"I call it insane," I said, standing up. "And I'm not doing it."

"I wouldn't advise you to say no, Ryan," Cole said.

"Is that a threat?" I asked, incredulous.

Cole shrugged. "There's something you don't know." He said the words pleasantly, as if he were commenting on a sunny day.

And that's what chilled me.

He went over to a far door. He opened it.

A short-haired woman with glasses was sitting on a hard-backed chair. She was dressed in jeans and a sweater that looked as though she'd slept in it for a week.

Maybe she had. It was Mom.

19//old king cole

I launched myself at Cole. I swung a fist, and it connected with his jaw. Cole reared back, surprised and in pain. But within seconds he had my arms pinned behind my back. I never said I was macho.

"Calm down, Ryan," he said. "Your mother just showed up at the gate this morning."

"You slime!" I cried, twisting. "Liar!" A red haze was in front of my eyes. I twisted in his grip, trying to get a hand free to smash him again.

"Ryan!" Mom hurried into the room. "Let him go, Coleman," she said.

Cole didn't flinch. He kept me pinned.

"I said, let him go," Mom said in a quieter tone. "He won't try that again. Will you, Ryan? Cole is telling the truth. He didn't kidnap me," she added. "I'm here of my own free will. Okay?"

Puzzled, I looked at her. She nodded at me reassuringly. My muscles went slack, and Cole dropped my arms.

He rubbed his jaw. "Quite a punch, for a computer nerd."

"Mom, what are you doing here?" I asked. I had to stop myself from rubbing my hand. It was throbbing. Nobody tells you that throwing a punch hurts just as much as getting one. "How did you know I was here?"

"It's a long story," Mom said. Then she took a quick step forward and hugged me. She cradled me against her as though I were still a baby. I didn't mind at all. I felt like a little kid. I felt as though now that my mom was here, everything would be all right.

"Well," Mom said, wiping her eyes as she finally let me go, "I guess I should start at the beginning. First of all, I knew Coleman years ago. We were in college together. Later, we worked together. Along with your father."

"I knew your dad, Ryan," Cole said. "I was his best friend."

"Liar," I said.

"It's true, honey," Mom said in a quiet voice. She took my hand. "Let's sit down. I'll tell you everything. It's time you knew."

We sat down on the bench under the window. Cole sat at his desk. I wished he would leave, but I knew better than to ask him.

"It was the two names, Jeremy and GuildMaster," Mom said. "They kept playing Ping-Pong in my head. I knew Jeremy as a baby, you see. And then I put that together with GuildMaster and Coleman. He was a medieval history major in school. So I contacted some people, and learned more about the Caravan."

"That seems like a pretty far-out connection," I said doubtfully. "Who would you know to contact? Why would you think that this history major was an underground computer guru/terrorist?"

"I'm not a terrorist, Ryan." Cole's voice was like a whip.

"Whatever," I said. I shot him a look full of hate.

"That's the hard part of the story," Mom said. Her voice suddenly wobbled, and her eyes filled with tears.

"Mom?" I watched as a long, slow tear dripped down her face. It fell off her chin and landed on her jeans. She rubbed at the damp spot.

She took a deep breath. Then she looked back up at me. "You see, I'm in the underground, too."

My whole face went slack in a classic *duh* expression.

Life certainly has a way of hitting you, doesn't it? It can smack you so hard that you spin around like a top.

"Y-You're . . . ," I stammered, but my mind was slowly starting to work again. Things clicked. Suddenly I had a whole new perspective on the past, and it made sense for the first time.

All our moves, I thought. Every year, for so long. Cincinnati. Minneapolis. Wilkes-Barre. Chicago. Nashville. Baltimore . . .

It hadn't been wanderlust. It hadn't been a fear of commitment. It hadn't been a spirit of adventure.

We'd been on the run.

"What did you do?" I asked her. "Why did you have to disappear? Did you rob a bank? Bomb a school?" I asked sarcastically. Mom flinched, as if I'd punched her, too.

"She didn't do anything," Cole said. "She fought for what she believed in."

I whirled on him. "I'm not talking to you," I spit out fiercely.

"In college, I got involved in the environmental movement," Mom broke in. "After graduation, your father and I got married and moved to Northern California. We were hired as fund-raisers for an organization called Green Alert. We opposed the major logging companies up there. The redwoods were being destroyed. I was working on a compromise position so that people wouldn't have to lose jobs. The lumber companies were scaring people, saying they'd pull out, that they'd close mills. So everyone got stirred up. Things got ugly."

Mom sighed. Cole sat straight in his chair, watching her with his pale gaze. I couldn't believe that they'd known each other before, had been friends.

"Coleman was working for the same organization," Mom said. "We'd do things like chain ourselves to trees to save them." She shrugged. "It seems like so long ago now."

"It's not that long ago, Allie," Coleman said. "The spirit is still alive. It's right here, in this place."

"Allie?" I said. "Your name is Grace."

"My name was Alice Sloane," Mom told me. "I changed it when I went underground."

I felt all turned around now. Nothing was the way I thought it was. Not even my own mother.

"Alice Sloane was the most famous environmentalist on the West Coast eighteen years ago," Cole said.

"I was part of a movement, that's all," Mom said, dismissing Cole's words with a wave of her hand.

"So what happened? Why did you have to go underground?" I asked.

"Things got really tense," Mom said. She rubbed the bridge of her nose in the way she did when she was really tired. "On one protest, people threw rocks at us. Trucks would cruise by our house late at night, just to let us know that they knew where we lived," she said, watching me carefully. "The pressure was on—they wanted us to close shop, leave town. And then . . ."

"And then?" I prompted.

Mom sighed. She pushed her hands through her short, dark hair. For the first time, I wondered what the real color was. She had dyed it at home for as long as I can remember, saying she was turning gray prematurely. But it must be a different color, maybe even blondish red, like mine.

"A lumber company's headquarters was bombed," Mom continued. "A man was killed—a bookkeeper working late. The three of us—Cole, Jack, and me—were called in for questioning. We told them we had nothing to do with it."

Mom looked at Cole. "Even though I suspected that you knew something."

Cole gave her an easy smile. "That's funny. I felt the same about you and Jack."

"There was a grand jury investigation, and we were all called to testify," Mom said, rubbing her nose again. "We went in the same car. Jack was driving. We were arguing about something stupid—Jack wanted to take this shortcut, and Coleman said we'd hit traffic, but Jack took it, anyway. And we were caught in this big traffic jam, and they started arguing again. . . ."

Mom's voice got weak. She dropped her head in her hands. She took a long breath and lifted her head again.

"I was sitting in the backseat, with Coleman," she whispered. "The front seat was broken, and we'd piled all our legal briefs and documents on it. Your father was a lawyer, Ryan. I never told you that. He was going to defend us. Anyway, the bomb . . . went off. They told me later that Coleman was blown out the back window. He went back for me. He got me out. But Jack . . ."

Mom closed her eyes. She pressed her fingers against her eyelids. "I haven't talked about this in so long. Ever."

"Allie—" Cole said.

But she held up her hand. "Let me finish it. Your father was in the driver's seat,

Ryan. The bomb was under the front seat. He died instantly."

"You told me he died in a car accident," I said. And I guess he did.

"Coleman and I were rushed to the hospital," Mom went on in a numb voice. "I just had a concussion. Some bruises, cuts from the glass—it was a miracle, they said. They told me Jack was dead. And then the police told me that they were going to charge me with murder for transporting the bomb."

Mom slipped her hand in mine and squeezed it. But I think she was holding it not to comfort me, but herself.

"I knew something they didn't. I was pregnant. And I knew, somehow, that I hadn't lost you, Ryan. I just knew. And I also knew that I had to save you, and myself. So I just walked out. They posted a guard, but he wasn't very vigilant. They didn't expect me to walk, since I was so weak. Escaping was easy. Staying free was the hard part."

"How did you do it?" I asked.

Mom shrugged. "Friends. Good friends. They got me an ID, got me relocated. Lily

. . . was one. Then it was up to me. I did the best I could, Ryan. Because you were always the most important thing. My parents, Jack's parents, were dead. We had that in common. We always said that if we had a child—we'd raise him together, no matter what." Mom's voice cracked again.

My thoughts were so confused, I couldn't fix on one of them. Mom had been this environmental activist terrorist. My dad had been blown to bits. And Cole had saved my mother's life.

"That morning," Mom said, "when the FBI showed up at our door? I thought they'd found me at last."

That explained how nervous she'd been. How strangely she'd acted. And why she'd wanted to get me out of town, fast. Because if the FBI started digging, who knew how deep they would go?

Cole leaned forward, his hands on his knees. "And now your mother has come to join us, Ryan," he said.

"*What?*" I exclaimed. I shot to my feet.

Mom looked down at her hands. "I respect Coleman very much, Ryan," she said. "I investigated what he had to say. I came to see what he was doing. I've been here all morning, and I have to say, I'm impressed with what I see. He's doing good things." She smiled at Cole. "It's like the old days."

"I thought you'd feel that way, Princess," Cole said.

Princess? I shot Mom a disbelieving look.

"An old nickname," she said quickly. "We used code names back in the old days. From a fairy-tale book I had. Your father— Jack—was Giant Killer. And Cole was Old King. Not very hard to crack," Mom added with a high little laugh that sounded strange.

I felt my world blow apart. Just when I thought I couldn't accept one more weird, crazy twist, it came zinging in my direction. I realized that I had reached ground zero. In a world where no one could be trusted, I couldn't even depend on my *mom*.

Mom wasn't here to rescue me. She was here to join them!

I whirled on her. "This is great. This is fantastic. This is what I've been leading to, my whole life. What have you always told me when we moved every year?" I mimicked her sweet motherly tone. "'This is teaching you independence, Ryan. But independence only goes so far. You can't let yourself get closed off. You've got to keep your heart open. You've got to trust people.'" I spoke normally again. "I tried, for a while. But just when I started to make a friend, you yanked out that magic carpet again, and I found myself living a thousand miles away!"

Mom started to cry. But I didn't care.

"But look at me now," I said. "I can't even trust my own mother! And do you know what, Mom? *I'm not surprised!* That's how messed up I am!"

"Ryan," Mom pleaded. "Listen to me—"

"Did he tell you what he wants me to do?" I asked her furiously. "He wants me to impersonate someone, steal passwords, plant this Millennium Virus—"

"Not a virus," Cole said sharply. "It's a warning beep."

"It's a virus!" I shouted. "This is the guy you think is doing *good things?*"

"Ryan, calm down," Cole said sharply.

Mom spoke to me softly. "Ryan, he saved my life once. I owe him something."

During my entire childhood, whenever I had gone off the deep end or had a fit, Mom had had this technique. She'd just keep talking in a low voice, so that I had to stop shouting to hear her.

But I didn't want to hear. Not anymore.

"No," I said. "You owe him nothing!"

But she kept talking. "We have to think about what the right thing to do is. And it might not be the clearest thing. I've made a bargain with Cole. If you do this one thing, he'll fabricate new identities for us. We can disappear again."

"But I don't want to disappear again!" I cried. "I'm tired of disappearing! I feel like I don't exist anymore!"

Tears ran down Mom's face. She grabbed my hand and squeezed it so hard that I felt my bones come together.

"Listen to me, Chiquita," she said. "This is the right thing to do."

My brain was whirling, but that one word made it slowly wind down. *Chiquita.*

Make like a banana and split . . .

Mom was telling me that we had to leave!

She was only pretending to go along with Cole. She hadn't meant it!

We exchanged a long glance. I saw that I'd guessed right. I nodded at her.

Now, I would have to acquire some acting skills, and fast. I relaxed my shoulders into a slump. I tried to look resigned.

I turned to Cole. "I guess I have no choice," I said. "How do I start?"

20//smithereens

Cole took my agreement with the same bland smile that he had taken in the world.

"I'll set you up with Komodo for encryption lessons," he said. "You're scheduled to start your job tomorrow."

"Tomorrow! I can't learn enough by tomorrow!" I cried. "I'll get caught for sure."

"Relax, Ryan," Cole said, putting a hand on my shoulder. "We know what we're doing. Komodo can teach you enough to fake your way through the first day. You'll pass through all the security checks, so you should be able to access the passwords. I've got your ID here, and a new laptop. You can store the passwords on here."

He slid a state-of-the-art laptop toward me along the desktop. "We only have the best here. And it's been souped up by Caravan members. This baby will rock." He stroked the top of it. For a man who was supposed to be afraid of technology, he sure got his jollies from hardware. "I have the same model."

Cole stood up. "Let me find Komodo. We'll start right away. And I think you and your mom deserve a few minutes alone." He headed out, shutting the door softly behind him.

As soon as the door closed, Mom put a finger to her lips. I hadn't thought of it before, but the place might be bugged.

"Will you look at this laptop?" I said, flipping it open. "It is so amazingly cool."

I tapped on the keys and wrote:

So how do we get out of here?

"I would expect Cole to only use the best," Mom said.

She wrote:

I have no idea.

No idea?

"At first I didn't buy it," I said. "But I have to admit that certain things Cole says make sense."

I wrote:

I thought you had a plan!!!!!

Mom shrugged. She wrote:

I just wanted to find you. I thought I'd figure the rest out once I got here.

Good thinking, I wrote, and made a face at her.

"It's not that I think we should join the Caravan, Ryan," Mom said. "At least, not yet. But I don't think we should interfere with it. We can do our bit to help, then move on."

If he lets us, I wrote.

We looked at each other. I could see the same fear in her eyes. But she leaned over to tap out a new message.

Don't worry. We'll make it out. Together.

The door opened, and we both jumped. I quickly hit the power button, and the laptop shut off. But it was only NancE, the frizzy orange-haired woman with the habit of twitching her nose like a rabbit.

"Cole says to head over to quad A—no, D, site 3," NancE said. "He set up the meeting with Komodo."

I nodded. "Okay. But—"

But NancE shut the door on my words. She was in a hurry, as usual. I wanted to ask her directions to site 3. Quad D was a maze.

I'd just have to find it myself. I picked up the computer.

"Here we go," I told Mom.

"24/7," she said.

"24/7," I told her.

I headed down the hall toward quad D, but I got turned around. The lights were dim in the corridors and there was no natural light, so it was easy to get confused. Especially since I wasn't exactly sure where I was coming from. I'd never been to Cole's private site before.

I stopped, trying to get my bearings. I had a feeling that I was near Jeremy's studio. The studio was in quad C, which was totally devoted to storage. D was next to C. But did I need to go right, or left?

I went left. I edged past a heap of old computer equipment and wires and into a narrower hall. The light was dim, and I had to feel the doors in order to read the numbers. My fingers followed the straight lines of a number one. Next door, I followed the curve of a two. Then a three. I turned the knob, and the door opened.

More computer equipment. I was in the wrong quadrant. This was the storage wing.

I closed the door. Maybe the quads linked up at the rear of the compound. Besides, it was one of the few times I had been able to wander around alone. Somehow, someone always swung into step beside me. Why hadn't that occurred to me before?

I felt the numbers on the next few doors. I found a four, and a five. But when I felt the next door, my fingers only found smooth wood. There was no number.

Maybe it had fallen off. But I was curious. I tried the knob. Locked. I felt under the knob and discovered that this door had a slot, not a keyhole. Now I could see the tiny red light that meant the door was locked.

I was out of luck. I couldn't even try to jimmy the lock.

And then I remembered the white plastic card I'd found in the truck bed. It was still in my pocket. I fished it out, then slid it into the slot. The light glowed green, and I heard a click.

I pushed open the door. It was pitch black inside the room. Even with the dim light from the hall, all I could make out were shadows. I felt along the wall. My heart thumped like a boom box with the bass turned up all the way.

I found the switch and turned on the light, then quickly shut the door.

I let out the breath I was holding. It was just more storage. Metal shelves were pushed against the walls. Canvas covered the items. Probably cans of food and fuel. Jugs of water. There wasn't even poured concrete on this floor, just hard-packed dirt.

I lifted up one of the canvas sheets, just to check.

I gasped, then clapped my hand over my mouth. I was staring at a pile of guns.

I lifted up another corner of sheet. Then another. And another, and another, and another, until I had looked on every metal shelf in the room.

There were enough automatic weapons here to blow all of New Mexico to smithereens.

So much for Cole's peaceful revolution.

I thought about taking a gun. But I was no Rambo. Where would I hide it? What would I do with it? I shook my head. If I was going to get out of here, I'd have to use my best weapon—my brain.

I noticed a clot of dirt on the side of my shoe, and brushed it off. I wouldn't want Cole to notice it.

The dirt was the same color as the dirt in the back of the truck. Thoughtfully, I prowled around the room. I didn't know what I was looking for, but I couldn't leave yet.

In the left corner, I noticed that the dirt was scored with long, deep slashes. As though the shelves had been moved recently.

Using all my strength, I pushed the unit away from the wall. Set into the floor was a wooden trapdoor. I expected it to be locked, but it moved. Nervously, I lifted it. I peered down into the darkness.

It was a tiny cubbyhole. There was a tarp on the floor, and a tin plate. Scraps. No Scud missiles or bombs. Disappointed, I let the trapdoor fall.

I pushed the unit back again. Then I forced myself to wait until I was breathing normally again. I wiped the sweat off my face with the tail of my shirt. Then I slipped out of the room and closed the door.

I studied encryption coding until my eyes were crossed. Komodo and I didn't even break for dinner—Sona brought us sandwiches and sodas. But finally, sometime after midnight, Cole stuck his head in the cube and called a halt.

"Are you serious?" Komodo asked. He had not shown the slightest sign of fatigue over the past seven hours. Every so often he would crack his knuckles for relaxation.

"Dead serious," Cole said. "He's got to be fresh. He's due there at eight A.M., and it's a two-hour drive. Is he ready?"

"He's ready," Komodo said. "I hit all the high spots. He should be able to fake it."

Cole nodded and turned to me. "Feeling confident?"

"No," I said.

He ignored that. "Topcat will drive you down the mountain tomorrow," he told me.

"Bud got back right in time for dinner, so we have a working truck. If all goes well, you can leave the day after."

Why don't I believe you? Could it be because you've lied to me every step of the way?

"Allie—your mother—is going to hang out here tomorrow," Cole told me. "She wants to explore the compound. And it will give us more time to chat. I'll take care of her. Don't worry."

Which meant that Mom was insurance. If I tried anything funny, Cole would have her.

"Confidence is three-quarters of the game, Ryan," Cole told me. "That's the secret to winning."

And a cache of automatic weapons doesn't hurt.

I didn't respond. Cole looked pained, like I had disappointed him. But after a moment, he just said good night and split. I closed my notebook, said thank you to Komodo, and headed toward my cube.

I knew I was stuck. Tomorrow, I would have to follow through on Cole's plans. What if I tipped off the FBI and Coleman made an Alamo last stand here? What if everyone picked up guns and started blasting away? What would happen to Mom?

I stopped. I was alone in the corridor. Suddenly, I felt that I couldn't take one more step. I couldn't move any farther in the direction I was going.

It was now or never. I had to think of a plan. I had to take a risk.

It was late, but the compound still hummed. I knew that Coleman would be still awake.

I knocked on his cube door, and he called, "Come in." He was sitting at his desk, working on his PC. His laptop was closed, right near his elbow.

"We haven't talked about something," I said. "Like, what if I get caught?"

He sighed and tapped a few keys. "You won't get caught."

"But what if I *do?* What should I say? Do you have a plan for getting me out? Or is your genius for organization limited to getting people into trouble?" I moved closer to the desk.

He spun around on his chair. Good. I

moved closer. I was starting to know Cole better. He was good at hiding his emotions. He rarely seemed angry, or even peeved. But things got to him.

"I was going to go over this tomorrow, but so be it," he said in a weary voice, as though I were a naughty child demanding attention. "Deny everything. Continue to insist that you're David Wallaby—"

"Even if they have his fingerprints?" I demanded. "Or they get a photo? It can't be that hard. They can expose me in about three seconds."

"Do you know, Ryan, how dangerous it is to program yourself for disaster?" Cole said disapprovingly. "You have to visualize success or you fail. Even the impossible is achievable if we—"

"Can the lectures, guru," I said. "You know why I'm doing this for you."

Now I'd really gotten to him. I slid my laptop onto his desk and jammed my hands into my pockets. "You've got my mom," I said. "So I'll do the job. It's not like I have to rob a bank with a machine gun, or anything. I just have to hack a few numbers.

But that doesn't mean I have to listen to you lecture me, okay? Especially when I have your number." I tried a stab in the dark. "Especially when because of you, my father is dead."

I saw color high on Cole's cheeks, as though someone had painted him, like a doll. His mouth went slack. I was happy to see that constant smile disappear.

"Maybe we should continue this discussion tomorrow," he said tightly.

I reached over for the laptop and slid it off the desk. "Fine with me."

And I walked out. I'd finally succeeded in rattling Cole, which was a bonus. But I'd also achieved what I'd come for. I had his laptop.

21//steal the world

I didn't have much time. I knew that. Any moment he could boot up the laptop at his elbow and discover that it wasn't his.

I turned out my lights and flung myself on the futon. I flipped open the laptop. The glow of the blue screen was all the light I needed. I clicked into the file manager program and scrolled. From what I could tell, the files dealt with accounting and supplies—the cost of running the compound. Nuts-and-bolts stuff.

I clicked on a few of the files. They were basic boring stuff—how many sacks of cornmeal they ordered in January, how many cans of kerosene . . .

I kept scrolling. I stopped at a directory called C *quad*.

C quad—where the supplies were kept. Including weapons.

It was probably just an inventory. But I clicked on it, anyway.

A box flashed on screen. I needed a password!

I hit the mattress in frustration. So far, all I'd discovered was the compound's voracious appetite for cornmeal. Beyond the password, the truly sensitive material must lie.

I closed my eyes, trying to think. I needed a password. Something Cole said all the time, or a nickname?

I typed in *Jeremy.* Nothing.

Sabrina. Nada.

millennium. Zilch.

Then I tried combinations of the above. Still nothing.

I had to do it! I had to find it! I was starting to work up a truly intense hatred of Cole. I thought of the way he looked at Mom, as if they were actually friends. When he had called her Princess, I really thought I'd lose it.

I froze. Then I leaned over and typed in:

oldking

And I was in.

There were only two files. I clicked on the first one, called *millplan*.

I had to read fast. I couldn't linger over each word. But I didn't have to. I got the gist of it in about ten seconds of scrolling.

Here was the biggest lie of all.

Cole wasn't planning to just scare the world. And he certainly wasn't planning to save it.

He was planning to steal it.

He had no intention of giving back control. I read with slowly mounting horror a detailed plan of Caravan-engineered computer foul-ups.

Blackouts over Texas, New Mexico, and Arizona. The foul-up of flight information in all major airports. The crash of the biggest online provider services. Sudden gibberish where numbers used to be in the files of the nation's largest banking chain.

So that when Cole revealed on January 1, 2000, that he had control of the nation, everyone would believe him. And if they didn't—

An air disaster, *preferably a large com-mercial aircraft like a 777 near a major city.*

Blackouts of Washington, D.C., New York City, Los Angeles, Chicago, and Miami.

And then everyone would know just how deadly serious he was.

I closed the file and just sat there for a moment, shaking. The notebook hummed in my lap. It was like a bomb ticking.

This time, I clicked on *mail.*

There were dozens of entries to an address called Dano50H. It was someone I'd never met, but I'd heard his name around. I didn't have much time left, so I clicked on an e-mail from two weeks earlier, a letter from Dano50H to GuildMaster.

GMaster,

Captive has gone on a hunger strike. Refusing food until we release. Procedure?

Captive? It couldn't be me. A month ago, I'd been snoring my way through senior year. Not to mention that the notion of me on a hunger strike was pretty far-fetched. I'd been shoveling in Sona's food since I'd arrived.

I clicked on Cole's reply.

Enforcer,

Let's give him a day or so. He'll cave. So to speak.

The date of the next e-mail was two days later.

GMaster,

Captive still holding out. He's weaker. Running a fever.

Cole's reply:

Enforcer,

Promise him release if he eats. Tell him we won't release him looking ill. Would go worse with us if we're caught.

The reply was the next day:

Gmaster,

He took some broth. We broke him. But time is running out. Maybe we acted too soon. We should have set up details of the recruitment project first.

Cole's reply:

Enforcer,

NO SECOND GUESSING. We had to move when we did. Media scanning paid off yesterday. Calling gen meeting.

I looked at the date. It was the day after

the article had appeared about me in the paper. The next letter was dated a few days later.

Enforcer,

Subject contacted online. Setup completed?

And the reply the same day:

GMaster,

It's a go.

I looked at the date. The next day, I'd met the McDoogles and started traveling cross-country with Jeremy. She was bringing me to them. The next letter was dated a week later.

Enforcer,

Captive still refusing cooperation. Good news is that there's still no reports of his disappearance back in WA. He thinks parents are arranging ransom.

WA—Washington. I suddenly realized who Captive must be—David Wallaby! They hadn't sent him to Thailand at all. They had imprisoned him somewhere. Maybe even somewhere in the compound!

I clicked on the next letter.

GMaster,

Trouble in NM means accelerated schedule, which can be good for us. Catcher should arrive late today.

The next letter was dated the day after I'd arrived at the compound:

Enforcer,

Keeping captive is risky. Let's try on possible scenarios such as overdose, suicide, etc. Send back three best scenarios. Problem should disappear.

Disappear? What did that mean? Did the Enforcer and Cole murder David Wallaby?

Enforcer,

Catcher needs reassurance. I'm allowing him full access to compound. MOVE CAPTIVE TONIGHT.

And the reply:

GuildMaster,

Captive moved.

I remembered the trapdoor and the cubbyhole. The tarp. The tin plate. I remembered the shovels in the back of the pickup.

I shuddered. Had Dano buried David Wallaby?

I looked at my watch. I had to finish.

Cole could be dropping by any minute. I clicked on the last e-mail entry.

GMaster,

What about Princess? Procedure?

I swallowed. My fingers were shaking so badly, I could barely click on Cole's reply.

Enforcer,

Same as Captive.

I dug into the briefcase I'd been given as "David Wallaby." I shook out a floppy disk. I plunged it into the A drive. Then I started to download.

The computer made grunting noises as the information traveled to my disk.

Then I heard footsteps. Someone was heading down the corridor.

I gazed at the floppy, willing it to hurry and grab every bit it could. The footsteps drew closer. I thought I recognized the sound of Cole's hiking boots. No one could walk as softly in those clunkers as Cole.

I whipped out the floppy and tossed it under my pillow. I turned off the laptop, slammed it shut, and slid it across the floor along with the briefcase. Then I jumped underneath the coverlet, shoes and all. I closed my eyes.

The door creaked open.

"Ryan?" Cole said.

22//trust

The light went on. I blinked, pretending to awaken.

"What? Is it time to go?" I said.

Cole strode into the room. He snatched up the laptop.

"Looks like we switched by mistake," he said, placing mine on the floor.

"Switched what?" I said, trying to sound groggy.

His pale eyes searched my face. I pretended to yawn. I felt as though I were in a cheesy sci-fi movie from the fifties, the kind with everyone wearing aluminum foil space suits. Cole was the bad guy from Planet X who could read minds.

He can't read your mind, I told myself. *Relax.*

So I waited him out. I didn't drop my

gaze. I practiced sending back Cole's own patented bland expression.

"Well, good night, then."

I lay back down and closed my eyes. "Good night."

It seemed to take forever. But he switched off the light and closed the door.

I bounded up as soon as his footsteps retreated down the hall. I flipped open my laptop and powered it up. Then I slipped the floppy into the drive.

But just then I heard a noise, and looked up. I saw the gleam of the doorknob across the room as it turned. It was too late to turn off the computer. The door opened, and it was Jeremy.

"I came to say good-bye," she said.

She slipped into the room and closed the door behind her. She hurried over to the futon and sat next to me.

"I waited for Dad to leave. What are you doing?" she whispered.

"Just going over some things for tomorrow," I said.

"I knew we wouldn't be alone tomorrow," she said. "I wanted . . . I mean, we might not get a chance to say good-bye again."

She'd lied to me. Was she lying to me now? Was the sadness in her eyes an act?

Would I be the biggest chump in the world to believe that she cared?

I was wound so tight that all my senses seemed as sharp as a wolf's. I could smell the perfume of her hair drifting near my shoulder. I could see the honey gleam of her skin. I could even, I thought, feel her sadness and confusion hit me like a draft of wind.

She doesn't know, I thought. I put together everything I knew about her, everything she was, and I was certain of that. She had no idea that her father was crazy. That he wanted to steal the world.

Trust. What did it mean? I could look it up in the dictionary. But I'd never felt the meaning of it the way I felt it at that moment. Because I'd never realized what it really, truly meant: risk.

Jeremy had installed herself into my heart and brain, as complex and beautiful and mysterious as the most elegant software. Maybe it hadn't been stupid of me to let that happen. Maybe, no matter what, it had been good. Even if she'd lied, my feeling had been pure. For the first time, I knew I had a heart. Wasn't that good?

And maybe if I trusted her now, even if she let me down, it would still be the right thing. Because I would open my heart to her. I would say, *Here it is. Take it.*

And she would do what she would do.

Maybe Rambo would have broken back into the storage room and taken fifty automatic weapons and blasted his way out. But suddenly, I understood what Mom had been trying to tell me.

True courage is risking your heart.

"Ryan, what is it?"

I guess I was staring at her like a ghost. Her eyes searched my face, just as Cole's had earlier. But there was a difference. Her eyes weren't cold. They glowed.

I bent over and kissed her. Her lips curved under mine in surprise.

"I have to tell you something," I said. "About your father."

##

So I told her everything. She didn't believe me, of course. She was shaking her head at the jump. But I kept talking, her head started to droop, and pretty soon, she was staring at her sneakers.

"I don't believe you," she whispered when I was finished.

"I'll show you," I said. I accessed the file in the floppy and tilted the screen toward her.

I saw the light change on her face as the file flashed on screen. Her eyes moved across the blue screen.

"This is your proof?" she asked. "Ryan, it's gibberish."

I grabbed the computer and tilted it toward me. She was right. Cole had encrypted the file so that it was impossible to transfer it.

I thought back to my encryption lesson. Cole could have planted something in his own file so that he'd know I accessed it. The file could eat itself as a response.

In other words, all the evidence could be gone.

Jeremy stood up. "I think you're trying to get me on your side," she said. "Look, Ryan. If you don't want to go tomorrow, nothing bad will happen to you or your mom. You're being paranoid."

"What about the guns?" I asked suddenly. "What about all the weapons I found?" I had forgotten to tell her about that detail. "They're in the storage quad. In the room without a number."

She looked uncertain. "You found guns?" She tossed her hair behind her shoulder. "So what? A few rifles, for hunting, if we run out of food—"

"Not rifles. Automatic weapons," I said. "Major ones. And lots of them. Enough for an army."

Jeremy looked confused. "Are you sure?"

I didn't bother to answer. "I'll show you. But, Jeremy, we don't really have time. We have to get out of here!"

"I won't go." Her jaw was set stubbornly. "I don't believe you!"

"Jeremy," I said desperately, "it's like the water fountains in high school, remember? There's something here that makes you go along. Makes you think things are cool when they're not. You have to think for yourself—do you really, truly believe that Cole wants you to?"

For a moment, Jeremy's face was a blank. Then, it just crumpled. I saw all the denial *whoosh* out.

"Do you mean, it's all really true?" Her voice sounded like a little girl's. "He's going to crash a plane, and he kidnapped David Wallaby, and he might have . . . killed him?"

"I swear," I said. "Jeremy, we've got to get out of here."

"I'll get the keys to the truck," she said.

"I'll get Mom," I said.

"Can you trust her?" Mom asked me when I woke her up and told her we were leaving. She said the words close to my ear as we spoke in whispers. "This whole place runs on mind control. She might still be under his influence."

"Mom, I don't know if I can trust her," I said. "And it doesn't matter. I'm going to take the chance."

The door cracked open, and Jeremy

slipped inside. "I have the keys," she whispered. "Follow me."

We crept through the maze of corridors, moving fast and silently.

"Where are you going?" I whispered to Jeremy. "The back door is the other way."

"There's another door," she told me in a low voice. "My father showed it to me, in case something happened and we had to split, fast. Only he and I know about it."

I nodded, and Jeremy moved ahead. She headed into quad C. We hurried past the closed doors of the storage rooms, past the room filled with guns. At the end of the corridor, she whipped out a card from her pocket. It was the same kind of magnetic stripe card that opened the weapons room.

She slid it into the slot and pushed open the door. She motioned me and Mom through.

We stepped inside a dark space. We couldn't see a thing. I felt Jeremy step in behind me and close the door.

Lights blazed on. Cole stood in the middle of the room.

"Looking for a midnight snack?" he said.

"Thank you, Jeremy," Cole said. "We must be careful not to lose our friends."

Jeremy went to stand next to him. So I had taken the chance, and lost.

"I saw her leave your room," Cole said to me. "She let me know the betrayal you were planning."

"Betrayal?" I said. "How can I betray you when I never agreed with you? You're forcing me to do what you want!"

"That is your interpretation," Cole said.

"Coleman, let us go," Mom said. "You'll find another way without Ryan's help. He's just a boy."

"He's a boy with a great mind," Cole said. "I don't want to see it wasted. He can help the world so much, Allie."

"How?" I said. "By taking it over? By

crashing computer systems? By crashing *planes?*"

Cole started. Shock made him whip his head around to me. I realized that Jeremy hadn't told him that I'd read his files.

Which meant that at least part of her was still on our side.

"I read your files," I said. "I copied them onto a disk."

"I don't think so," Cole said. "First of all, you need the password—"

"Old king," I said softly.

Cole looked rattled now. "And second, you can't copy the files—"

"I know, they're encrypted," I said. "But you forget what a good teacher I had. A little knowledge is a dangerous thing."

"You're lying!" Cole suddenly shouted. "Even Komodo can't break my code!"

"Fine," I said. "Whatever you say."

Cole took deep breaths to calm himself. Jeremy faded back until she was pressed against the wall. Her eyes stayed on her father.

"I'm sending you two with Bud," he said to me and Mom. "He'll watch over you, keep you comfortable. I've already made plans to move the compound. We're going to a new home. The others are packing up the equipment. It's time to go. It's all over."

I didn't know what to believe now. But through the closed door, I heard someone approach, whistling. I recognized the tune. It was the theme from *Hawaii Five-O*, that old TV show. Which meant it had to be Bud.

Wait a second. I had read Dano50H, the online address, as Dano-Fifty-H. But what if 50H meant Five-O? There was a character on the show called Danny. His nickname was Dano.

Bud was the Enforcer.

And now Cole was putting us in his hands.

"Jeremy, he's lying," I said desperately. "Bud is the one who either murdered David Wallaby or is going to. He knows what your father is really planning."

"Don't listen to him, Jeremy!" Cole shouted.

The door opened. Bud walked in. He was wearing a Hawaiian shirt with his black

Levis. He stopped and glanced at us. I saw a strange blankness in his eyes. I knew that we meant nothing, that he would dispose of us like a crumpled-up bag of potato chips.

"What do you want me to do with them?" he asked Cole.

"I think you should know something, Cole," I said. "Not only did I copy your files, I e-mailed them to the FBI."

Cole smiled. "Now I know that you're lying. No one can e-mail out of the compound but me. And I know you didn't figure out how to hack your way past that gateway. You didn't have time."

He had me there. I could bluff him, but he would know it. Then I remembered that Jeremy actually did know how to break into Cole's e-mail system. But I hesitated. If Cole knew that, what would he do to Jeremy?

"Search him," Cole said to Bud. "Get the disk."

Suddenly, Jeremy stepped forward. "Don't bother. I have it."

But she didn't. I had put the disk in the pocket of my denim jacket. I had to stop myself from slapping my pocket, to make sure it was still there.

Cole looked uncertain. "Jeremy?"

She walked over and slipped the disk into his computer. "And Ryan lied—he couldn't break your encryption. Let me show you."

She entered a few keystrokes. Cole stood behind her.

"What are you doing?" he asked. "That's my mail gateway."

"I know," Jeremy said. She typed in an address. Then she turned around and faced him. "All I have to do is press Enter," she said.

Cole watched her warily. "For what?"

"For the files to go to the FBI," she said. "I'm sure they have encryption experts."

Bud started toward her, but Cole held up his hand. "Don't, Bud."

"That's right, Bud," Jeremy said calmly. "Because my finger is on the Enter key. If you take one more step, I push." She didn't remove her gaze from her father. "You look nervous, Dad. That must mean that everything Ryan told me is true. Is it?"

Cole swallowed. "We should talk—"

"We should have talked earlier," Jeremy said.

"You don't understand," Cole said. "I'm a visionary, Jeremy. I see where the world is headed, and it's a dark place. I can prevent it. But people don't listen. Their minds are numb. They watch TV and read magazines and waste their time hopping from Web page to Web page, thinking they are taking part in a revolution when they are only treading water! While c-computers form a chain, link by link, that will b-bind us as completely as any ch-chain forged by man!"

Cole's voice was thundering now. But it shook, and he was starting to stutter.

"I was always the one who knew," he said, turning to Mom. "Wasn't I, Allie? Wasn't I the smart one? No one listened to me when I said we had to fight back. We had to make a stand, we had to show them we were just as powerful as they were. If the ends justified the means for them, we had to match them, blow for blow!"

"The bomb," Mom whispered. "You did bomb that office."

"I didn't think anyone would be there!" Cole cried. His eyes glittered with tears. "And the car bomb—I didn't mean for it to go off!"

Mom gasped. He took a step toward her.

"I didn't! It was Jack's fault! It was wired to go off while we were in the c-courthouse. I had planned it! It wouldn't have hurt anyone. But he had to take that shortcut. He always had to have . . . h-his . . . own way!" Cole forced out. "And I saved you, didn't I? I dragged you from the burning wreckage, and you never thanked me! Not once!" he screamed.

Cole whirled back to face Jeremy. "You see, Jeremy? I live with death and betrayal *every day*. Because I can. I'm strong enough. And I can live with other deaths, other betrayals. Because I'm above them. My mission is higher. I am going to save the world!"

I heard movement behind me. NancE was standing in the doorway. Next to her was Komodo. Behind him was Sona, and Topcat, and Quark, and the other workers I'd met. They were all staring at Cole as though they'd never seen him before.

"I know *the way*," he said to them. Tears coursed down his cheeks. "You know I do. Follow me. We are a guild, we are the past that is the future. We have to step forward. Step with me," he pleaded.

"Daddy, I'm sorry," Jeremy whispered. I saw her push the Enter key.

And Cole saw it, too. With a roar, he launched himself at her. I jumped toward her a split second later.

But Cole wasn't going after his daughter. He picked up the chair. He smashed it into the monitor. Jeremy jumped back, knocking into me.

Cole picked up another monitor and threw it down.

"I am not the source of evil!" he screamed.

He tore out a computer, wires dangling, and threw it across the room. "This is the source!"

I felt Jeremy press keys into my hand. "Go now," she told me rapidly. "The truck is in the driveway. Take your mother and go."

"Come with us," I said, over the sound of Cole screaming. Glass splintered as he threw a monitor on the floor.

Tears filled Jeremy's eyes. "I can't," she whispered.

"But he'll hurt you—"

She shook her head violently. "No," she told me. Her gaze was blue and bottomless, full of mystery and sorrow. Tears streamed down her face. "I've seen him like this before," she said.

She squeezed my hand around the keys. "Take her and go. He could hurt you."

The keys bit into my flesh. Still, she kept her hand around my hand, squeezing.

"I'll never forget you," she murmured. I barely heard her voice over the sound of Cole smashing the computers. But I heard every word.

I signaled to Mom, and we left the room. Everyone just stood frozen, watching Cole destroy what he'd built.

No one stopped us as we hurried down the twisting corridors. The front door was unlocked, and we stepped outside.

The night was deep and still. The fresh

scent of pine hit our nostrils as we walked to the truck.

I backed up and headed down the mountain. I drove carefully down the unfamiliar, rutted road. Finally, we hit a paved road, and I turned downhill. As we drove, we could see lights of Santa Fe spread out below us, guiding us.

We were halfway to the city when we heard the first sirens.

//epilogue

Cole tried to burn the place down. The toxic smoke from the tires rolled over the ponderosa pines and the piñon trees. But the fire trucks made it up there quickly. Only a portion of the compound was destroyed.

They found David Wallaby in an underground room dug deep in the forest. He was more dead than alive. But they got him to a hospital, and he pulled through.

Coleman Felice was charged with kidnapping and attempted murder, on top of his other crimes. His daughter, Jeremy Felice, was charged with computer crimes. So were all the other Caravan members except for Sona, who got a suspended sentence. Cole hadn't lied about the fact that she was only a good cook.

Bud McDoogle was charged with attempted murder. It turned out that he and Twyla had criminal records from way back. Their children were placed in foster care. I hope they found a good home.

I was in a little trouble with the FBI for a while. Jeremy had only managed to send the e-mail to the office. She hadn't sent the file that outlined Cole's plans. Naturally, the FBI wanted it, in order to build their case.

I told them I had trouble locating it. I couldn't quite remember what I'd done with it. Maybe my confusion was because of my long incarceration at the compound. And maybe it was because I was so worried about Mom. Even though we'd told them that Coleman had planted those bombs eighteen years ago, there were still charges held against Mom.

I wasn't the most popular person around the FBI office. But eventually, I handed over the disk, and they dropped the charges against Mom. Especially after I gave an interview to Barbara Walters describing my ordeal, and how brave my mom had been to walk into that compound, knowing that Cole was crazy.

They say that Barbara can make anybody cry.

I wrote to Jeremy in jail. I didn't say much. I just thanked her for saving us.

She wrote me back:

Dear Ryan,

Thank you for writing. It meant a lot to me. So did your friendship.

Have a good life. Don't take this wrong. But please don't write to me again. It's just too hard.

Love,

Jeremy

Mom decided that she needed a new name, to symbolize her new life. So she was now known as Grace Allison Sloane. And I became Ryan Jackson Sloane. She went back to her true hair color, which was like mine. Except that it was threaded with gray, so she ended up dyeing it again.

"And to think that all this time, I thought you were a winter, and you were really an autumn," I said. "No wonder I'm such a head case."

"New hair for a new life," Mom said as we packed up our house in North Carolina. She had decided to move to San Francisco to be near me. "We're going to have a normal life for a change. Or as normal as we can have, considering it's California."

No more lies in our future. No more running.

We knew that much. We didn't know much else.

But I knew one thing for dead sure. It's a lot easier to face your future when you've confronted your past.

danger.com

@5//Stalker/

b y
j o r d a n . c r a y

1//cool jump

"So what store do you want to hit first?" I asked Camille as we walked through the mall entrance.

She shrugged.

Here is an example of one of the things that drives me crazy about the new Camille. It's like any interest or enthusiasm is suddenly uncool. She communicates totally through shrugs, sighs, and eye rolls.

Normally, right about now, I'd make a crack about how Camille might want to test her vocal cords. But I wanted to start out on the right foot. For some totally insane reason, I actually thought we might have a good time that afternoon.

"How about checking out some new CD–ROMs at the computer store?" I asked.

Camille rolled her eyes. She sighed.

"Hey, I know!" I said in a fake cheery voice. "Let's check out the new saucepan display at the Kitchen Korner!"

"Are you totally in–*sane?*" Camille asked.

"I hear they have some new nonstick surfaces," I said. I was goading her. At least I'd gotten her to talk.

She gave a really deep sigh. "Let's check out Riot."

Riot is a store in the mall that sells trendy clothes on the principle that every teenager wants to look like every other teenager. They'll never go broke.

I avoid it on principle, but also because I'd feel stupid wearing what they sell. Call me crazy, but a skintight rubber dress with fluorescent-green racing stripes doesn't make me want to break out into a chorus of "I Feel Pretty." More like, "I Feel Like a Radial Tire."

We flipped through clothes in Riot while alternative rock music thumped in our ears. Camille held up a see–through lace blouse that came with a matching corset. "This is cute," she said.

"Perfect for church!" I approved.

She put it back and flipped lazily through the racks.

I followed behind her. "Isn't it seriously strange how they call it 'alternative rock' when they play it everywhere you go?" I asked.

"Are you going to start?" Camille asked me, her hand on her newly bony hip.

"Start what?" I asked.

"Because if you're going to start, I'm out of here," Camille said.

I wasn't sure what she meant, but I guessed I wasn't supposed to make conversation. So instead, I trailed behind her while she held up various items of clothing, shook them, then slipped them back in the rack. She didn't even bother asking me what I thought.

I held up a short–sleeved sweater I thought was cute.

Camille rolled her eyes. "Bo–ring."

"Actually, I was wondering what kind of boring person would wear this," I said, putting it back. "That's why I picked it up."

"Yeah, right," Camille said.

"Um, Camy?" I said, using her nickname deliberately. "There's this concept I want to introduce you to? It's called *irony*. All the smart people are using it. I realize this means that it hasn't reached your crowd."

Camille flipped her long dark hair over her shoulder. "Let's get something to eat," she said.

I shrugged, then nodded. I decided to become an instant freshman in the Camille Brentano Body Language School. As we walked to the food court, I felt a strange sensation, as if a Nerd Fungus was actually growing on my body.

"How about splitting a barbecued chicken pizza?" I suggested.

"I want a Skinni Freeze," Camille said, ignoring my suggestion.

"Yum," I agreed. "Air–injected nondairy chemicals always hit the spot."

Camille gave me a look. I guess it meant, *you're starting.*

So I stopped.

We walked over to the frozen yogurt counter. Camille ordered a vanilla nonfat with strawberries. I said I'd have the same.

The girl just stared at us for a minute. They do not recruit food court employees from M.I.T.

"What flavor did you say?" she asked Camille.

"Vanilla," Camille snapped. "Was my order too complicated for you?"

The girl's face seemed to implode. She was around our age, and had what my mother would call an "unfortunate" complexion. She gazed at Camille, her mouth open.

"With strawberries," I added. I smiled at her so that she wouldn't think both of us were rude.

But she didn't even look at me. She scurried away and hurriedly thrust a plastic dish under the big nozzle. Frozen yogurt began to spiral out in those big droopy logs.

"After this, you want to go kick some puppies?" I asked Camille.

"What's that supposed to mean?" she asked, fishing for her wallet.

"You don't have to treat everyone like dirt, you know," I said. "You can save it for the people who really deserve it."

Camille's hand stopped moving. Her head was down, and her hair hid her face. I couldn't see her expression.

"Oh," she mumbled. "I've got a lot on my mind today, Mina."

It was the first human thing she'd said all day. We paid the dumpy counter girl and walked to a table in silence.

I dipped a spoon into my yogurt. I let the coolness slide down my throat. Did I dare try to be nice to Camille? Would she just roll her eyes and tell me that concern was *lame?*

"Want to share it?" I asked.

Camille looked down at her yogurt in confusion. Sometimes, she's not the swiftest.

"Not your yogurt," I said softly. "What's on your mind."

"Oh." Camille picked off a strawberry and ate it. She was wearing baby blue nail polish.

"Do you ever chat online, Mina?"

"Not much," I admitted. "Most of the conthe good girl. Following the rules. You're such a loser!"

"I said I'd go," I protested.

"Like I need you," Camille said. "Like I need anyone." She pulled her purse off the chair. "I'm out of here."

"But I have the car!" I cried, hurrying around the table toward her.

She whipped her big purse over her shoulder, almost slapping me in the face.

"I'll take the bus," she told me, and strode off.

Camille should meet this guy at all. He sounded bogus. Why was he so interested in a high school kid?

Camille suddenly threw her napkin across the table. "Look, forget it. Just forget it. I should have known better." She stood up, her chair scraping loudly. The yogurt girl looked over at us.

"Calm down," I said to Camille. "I'll go, okay?"

Because if I didn't, Camille might go alone. And that would be worse.

"As long as it's in a public place," I added.

Camille put her hands on the back of the chair. She leaned toward me, her dark hair swinging. "I'm not going to meet him in his *apartment*, Mina. I haven't even talked to him on the phone yet. I'm not stupid, no matter what you might think."

"I don't think you're stu—"

"Mina's the smart one," Camille said in a high voice, as though she were mimicking someone. But I had no idea who it was. "If only Camy were quick, like Mina. If only she'd lose that weight."

"Camy—"

"Oh, screw it," Camille said. "You've always been such a wimp, Mina. Toeing the line, being

Mina, I forgot how cynical you are. I remember how it got on my nerves. As soon as I wanted to do something, you always shot it down."

The shaft from Camille's little bow and arrow hit its mark—*ping!* I felt hurt. I slurped some yogurt off my spoon.

"What about Mick?" I asked.

"What about him?" Camille snapped.

"I thought you two were supposed to be the perfect couple," I said. "Why are you cheating on him?"

Camille looked irritated. "I'm not *cheating* on him, okay? Just don't worry so much about my personal life."

"I'm not *worried*," I said, "it's just that—"

"Look, here's the deal." Camille leaned over the table. "Will you come with me when I go to meet him?"

I hesitated, surprised. Why was Camille asking me?

"You're the only one I can trust, Mina." *And I'm the only one who won't blab,* I thought, staring into Camille's crystal green eyes. *So it won't get back to Mick.*

But what did the reason matter? Camille was asking me for a favor. The only trouble was, it was a favor I didn't want to grant. I didn't think

"He said that because I won that contest, I could probably get an agent," Camille said.

Last month, Camille had won a Deva Winter look-alike contest. She actually looks a little like the nineteen-year-old actress, who was nominated this year for her first Academy Award. Deva Winter was shooting a movie south of Mohawk Falls down in Saratoga Springs, and the local chapter of the Deva Winter Fan Club had sponsored a contest. Camille had worn a wig, just like Deva's signature hairstyle, and had dressed just like her character in *Sensible Shoes*. She'd won a gift certificate for a Day of Beauty at Shear Heaven, this ultrahip salon.

"Andrew said I should cut my hair like Deva's when I go in for my haircut," Camille said. "I can't wait. I'm going next weekend."

"Why should you make yourself into a carbon copy of Deva Winter?" I asked. "That sounds like a stupid idea to me."

Camille ripped a napkin out of the holder and wiped her fingers. "What makes you such a Hollywood expert?"

"I'm not saying I'm an expert," I said carefully. "I'm just saying that Andrew might not be. How do you know he really writes screenplays?"

Camille gave me a cool look. "You know,

She put the bite in her mouth and smiled.

That's when I knew she was lying.

"How much older?" I repeated.

She swallowed. "Okay. He's twenty-seven."

"Twenty-seven? Camy, are you crazy?" I blurted. "That's way old for you."

"He says I'm really mature for my age," Camille said defensively.

"I'm sure," I said. "What do you think a twenty-seven-year-old man is doing hanging with a seventeen-year-old girl? Do the math, will you? The guy is a pervert!"

"Thanks a lot, Mina." Camille's face was stony. "You really think a lot of my judgment, don't you."

Well, I didn't want to get into that. After all, Camy was dating Mick Mahoney, whose brain had been cloned from Barney Rubble.

"It's not that, Camy," I said.

"Camille!"

"It's that you can't know what somebody's really like when you meet them online."

"I know what Andrew's like," Camille said stubbornly. "He's way more intelligent than any guy I've ever known. He really knows movies and show business. He says he can help me be an actress."

"Right," I said. "I'm sure he's Mr. Hollywood."

versations are so stupid. Maybe I can't find the right chat rooms, or something. The ones I click into seem full of every guy you don't want to talk to in your own high school."

"That's true," Camille said. She moved her spoon around in her yogurt, but she didn't take a bite. "But that's in kid chat rooms. There are some cool places to hang out in. Like, for instance, rooms where they just talk about movies."

"I guess that could be cool," I said. But I was imagining a bunch of guys talking about the latest action film and saying, "Awesome, awesome, awesome!"

She dabbed at her mouth with her napkin, even though she hadn't taken a bite yet. "Anyway, I kind of met someone."

"Kind of met?" I asked.

"I met someone, okay?" Camille said. "He's so cool. We've talked for hours and hours. His name is Andrew, and he's a writer."

"Does he write for his school paper?" I asked.

She made a face. "No, he doesn't do kid stuff. He writes screenplays. Actually, he's older."

"How much older?" I asked suspiciously.

"Twenty-four," Camille said, digging up a big spoonful of yogurt.